COLDWATER RANGE

COLDWATER RANGE

JOHN D. NESBITT

FIVE STAR
A part of Gale, a Cengage Company

LIBRARY OF CONGRESS CATALOGING-IN-PUBLICATION DATA

Names: Nesbitt, John D., author.
Title: Coldwater range / John D. Nesbitt.
Description: Waterville, Maine : Five Star, 2022. | Series: Five
  Star frontier fiction |
Identifiers: LCCN 2021040908 | ISBN 9781432889012 (hardcover)
Subjects: LCGFT: Western fiction. | Novels.
Classification: LCC PS3564.E76 C65 2022 | DDC 813/.54—dc23/
  eng/20211007
LC record available at https://lccn.loc.gov/2021040908

First Edition.
Find us on Facebook—https://www.facebook.com/FiveStarCengage
Visit our website—http://www.gale.cengage.com/fivestar
Contact Five Star Publishing at FiveStar@cengage.com

Printed in Mexico
Print Number : 2   Print Year : 2022

For Pal

CHAPTER ONE

Del Rowland leaned forward in the saddle as his horse loped to the top of the hill. He drew rein as the country came into view. A hundred yards down the slope, two men sat on horseback as their horses swished their tails. The low tone of voices carried on the air, but he did not make out any words. It was just as well. Whatever Overlin and Hardesty were discussing was their business. So he had learned in a hundred small ways.

Bill Overlin, boss of the Spoke, was wearing his characteristic brown hat, jacket, and matching trousers. He was seated on his zebra dun, a yellowish horse with black markings, and he wore plain brown riding gloves. Rich Hardesty, foreman of the neighboring Pyramid Ranch, was dressed in drab range clothes, a dull black hat, and a brown vest. He sat straight up on a shiny sorrel that bent its neck and was rubbing its foreleg. Del thought the two men must have seen him, but they gave no indication.

Motion caught Del's eye. At about the same distance downhill but fifty or sixty yards to the right, a brown horse was pulling tension on a rope, and a man was kneeling on the flank and neck of a dark brown calf. Del recognized the man, a fellow named Al Fisher, who rode for the Pyramid. In the same instant, Del wondered which outfit's brand, if any, lay under Fisher's hand as he rubbed the calf's side.

Fisher reached for the rope, gave a tug for slack, loosened the loop, lifted it from around the calf's neck, and stood up. The calf scrambled to its feet and bounded away.

Del had the uneasy feeling of not knowing how much he was supposed to have seen. The Pyramid Ranch lay on the other side of Coldwater Canyon, west and north of here, so Hardesty and Fisher seemed a ways off their range, though this was public domain and therefore open range. As a general rule, a cowhand didn't throw a rope on an animal unless it carried his outfit's brand, but if he did it under the watchful eye of another cattleman and his own foreman, he must be on the up-and-up.

Whatever the case, Del thought he should report to his boss, so he let his horse saunter downhill to the spot where the two men were talking. Their voices had gone quiet, and they watched him as he approached.

Overlin tipped his head up, and the sunlight fell upon his clean-shaven face, flushed and filling out in middle age. His brown eyes held on his hired man. "See anything?"

Del understood the question in its routine sense, to refer to his ride since leaving the ranch after the noon meal. "Nothin' to speak of."

"So much the better."

Del nodded at Hardesty, who returned the gesture.

The Pyramid foreman had a surly way about him, and he did not vary it now. He drew himself up straight, adjusted his reins in his gloved hands, and looked past Del. He had a muddy complexion, and his mouth turned down at the corners as if he disapproved of something. His wide, brown eyes had little expression, though his sparse mustache made a small twitching motion. His horse bent to rub its foreleg again, and Hardesty's large-roweled spurs made a faint jingle.

Del turned as Fisher came loping up on the brown horse, brought it to an abrupt stop, and settled. A small cloud of dry bits of grass drifted across the group.

Fisher was of average height or a little less, and he had his horse downhill a foot or so. He said, "It's a Spoke brand, all right. Just had some of the dead skin curling away and made it look like someone had tried to change it." Fisher wore a brown hat with a rounded crown, which he set back on his head, to reveal a pale complexion and dark brown, staring eyes. He gave a half-smile and spat tobacco juice off to the side. His mouth remained crooked when it relaxed.

Del remembered Fisher and his brand of humor from spring roundup, and he expected him to say something vulgar.

Fisher did not disappoint. "He had his nuts cut off. I checked that while I was at it."

Overlin looked away.

Hardesty said, "It's the brand-changin' that we're concerned about."

"Here's Mac," said Overlin.

Del turned in his seat, and his horse shifted. A rider was angling down the slope on a long-legged pale horse. Del recognized his fellow rider, Macmillan.

The group waited. Del's horse, a grey, nickered to the new arrival.

Macmillan drew the pale horse to a stop and faced the boss. Being above average height and slender, he sat tall in the saddle. He wore a dust-colored hat, off-tone with his wavy light brown hair and short beard. He wore a grey shirt, a brown cloth vest, denim trousers, and scuffed boots with spurs that had rowels the size of a two-bit piece. He took off his hat to wipe his brow, and a bald spot showed on the back of his head. He put on his hat and said, "Everything looks in order today." He turned to Del and said, "I thought we'd meet a little farther on, but this is all right, I guess."

Del shrugged. "I suppose. I just stopped here for a minute because I saw them."

Macmillan drew a white tobacco sack out of his vest pocket.

Overlin said, "Then you two must have work to do."

Macmillan slipped the sack into his pocket again. "That's right." His eyes met Del's. "Shall we go?" He nodded at Hardesty and Fisher and said, "Afternoon, fellas." Holding his reins high, he cued his horse and walked it away.

Del glanced around, said, "See you later," and fell in with his riding partner.

Neither of them spoke for several minutes. When they had put a low hill behind them, Macmillan said, "I hope I didn't ride into the middle of someone else's palaver."

"Not while I was there. Fisher had roped a calf to check its brand. Said it was a Spoke. I just happened by. I wasn't there but a minute when you showed up." Del had a sense that his boss did not like being observed by one of his men, much less two, but he said no more.

They rode on for a while until Macmillan spoke again. "Looka there. Someone cut down a tree."

They nudged their horses across a sidehill where the remains of a cedar tree lay in the first shadows of the afternoon. Someone had cut it down with an ax, had trimmed off the branches, and had cut off the narrow end where the thickness had tapered down to about four inches. The log, or future post, was about nine feet long. The trunk end would measure almost a foot across, and the red and cream-colored layers gleamed fresh.

Macmillan pursed his lips. "I'm sure they're comin' back for it."

"I imagine. But I'm sorry to see such a nice tree get cut down, when they're not all that plentiful."

"It's the way people do things. Public land. Everyone's used to free grass, free timber and firewood, free water—wherever they can get it."

"How old do you think it is?"

Macmillan raised his eyebrows and shrugged. "Oh, I don't

know. I'd say at least thirty. I've heard of trees bein' smaller than this one and being a hundred and fifty years old, but those are weathered, twisted, stunted old trees growin' in tough places. Of course, people cut them down, too. You see a lot of twisted fence posts."

"Well, I'm sorry to see this one go down. A good tree in its prime."

"That it is."

The two men rode on a little ways more, then split up again for the rest of their afternoon ride.

The corral posts were casting long shadows as Del slipped the halter off the grey horse and let it go. He walked back into the dusky barn, found the peg, and hung the halter. With the last task of the day, he was conscious of sticking to principle. Some of the other punchers tied their horses with the reins after a day's ride, but whether it was his gear and horse or the outfit's, Del did not want to risk breaking a set of reins. Some riders also turned out their horses without brushing them, just as some of them did not brush the horse ahead of time but ran a hand along the horse's back and under its chest before throwing on a saddle. Every time Del did things the way he thought he should, he reinforced doing things the way he had learned.

As he walked outside into the clearer, cooler air, a cheerful voice sounded on his left.

"Hey, puncher."

He paused and turned. The sight of Lawna, with her blond hair touching the shoulders of a light blue dress, made him smile. "Evenin'."

"Long day?"

"Normal."

"Last one out of the barn."

"Sometimes I take longer putting my horse away. Of course,

we don't always get in at the same time, either."

"I know."

He let his eyes drift over her. She did not seem to have made herself up in any special way, and he wouldn't have expected her to. He understood as common knowledge that she was more or less engaged to Rich Hardesty, so as a habit, he kept his conversation on a casual level and did not try to flirt. And even at moments like this one, when there seemed to be a bit of a spark or glow, he knew there would always be a distance between him and the boss's daughter, or stepdaughter. He did not feel he was being suggestive when he said, "What are you up to?"

"Just out for some fresh air."

"No harm in that."

"It gets so stuffy. Sometimes it seems as if the hot weather will never end."

"Maybe not all at once, but it will."

"I know."

"Time goes by. Next thing you know, it's cold and wet. Then cold and windy. Then just cold."

She raised a hand and brushed a strand of hair into place. "They say time goes by faster every year. Is it true?"

He had her placed at eighteen, which made him eight years older. He did not mind being treated as the one with more experience—after all, he had lived elsewhere and worked on other ranches. "I suppose it is. Unless you're sad and lonely, or you have a miserable job. Then time goes by at a crawl."

She took a deep breath, and her bosom perked. He made himself look away. Her voice brought him back.

"Is that the way it is with you?"

He shook his head to clear it and to remember what he had just said. "No, not at all. I'm not sad and lonely. No one has thrown me over of late. And I don't mind my place in life. I'd rather be a common ranch hand than work in a factory. As long as I can feel that I'm working to improve myself and I'm doing it in an honest way."

She tipped her head and regarded him with what seemed like interest. "You have it thought out, don't you?"

He shrugged. "I ought to have some sense of myself. Being so much older, you know."

She gave a light laugh. "That's how we learn. By talking to people who have been other places and seen other things."

"There are some ways that might be even more dependable."

She laughed again. "Like reading *Little Women?* Yes, reading is all right, but I save it for long winter days."

"I read *Robinson Crusoe* one winter when I was about twelve. I thought it was a true story until I found out otherwise."

"I had a Sunday school teacher who said all novels were wicked. It made me want to read some, but I found out she was wrong. Half the novels you read are about virtue triumphing over vice. In those words."

"Or about boys working hard. They start out shining shoes and end up working in a mercantile firm."

A bell rang from the direction of the ranch house.

"That's for me," she said.

"Good evening, then. It was good to see you."

"Yes, it was." She turned and walked away at a quick pace, her light blue figure making a pleasant image as it retreated in the dusk.

Tobacco smoke hovered in the lamplight of the bunkhouse as the after-supper relaxation set in. Macmillan was rattling silverware in the dishpan at the end of the long table, while Rucker, the cook, was banging skillets on the cast-iron stove in the kitchen. Price and Westfall, riding partners, sat across the table from Del. Halfway between Del and Macmillan, Bill Overlin sat smoking his pipe.

Price sat sideways on the bench, cleaning his fingernails with a penknife. He had his eyebrows raised as he studied his work, and the toothpick in the corner of his mouth stuck out like a stem of hay. He had a nonchalant, good-natured air about him, and he had his mouth pursed as if he was about to whistle a tune. Westfall, half a head taller, sat up straight facing the table with his chin tucked as he rolled a narrow cigarette. With his light-colored hair, pale eyes, thin face, spectacles, downy mustache, and sagging mouth, he had a morose expression, like that of an undertaker's assistant.

Overlin sat with his usual repose. His hat hung on a peg, and the overhead lamplight shone on his straight brown hair with a receding hairline and a tuft in the middle of a bald spot. Del was accustomed to seeing him in the evening when he would drop in for a while, smoke his straight-stem pipe, and seem quite at ease, even though he did not chum or fraternize with the men.

Price held up his hand with his fingers curled like a claw. "Now, that's better. One thing girls don't like, and that's dirty fingernails."

Westfall gave no response.

Macmillan said, "Washin' dishes is good for that. Gets your hands clean, and your nails, too."

Price's toothpick bobbed. "Except in cold weather. Then it makes your hands dry and rough. Girls don't like that."

Macmillan wagged his head. "That's why your sheepherders use mutton tallow, and your milkmaids use bag balm."

Del stole a glance at the boss, whose face had a strange, lifeless cast to it. As if he was aware of being observed, Overlin wrinkled his nose and turned down the corners of his mouth. He reached forward and rapped his pipe upside down in the heavy clay ashtray.

Silence held. The boss cleared his throat and said, "I think there's somethin' goin' on." With everyone's attention on him, he continued. "There's always been a problem with rustlers, more at some times than at others, and more in some places. I think there's some of that goin' on right now, on my range. Brandin' calves that got missed in spring roundup, changin' brands that aren't very old."

Del noted the wording. Overlin referred to his range as any place where he ran cattle.

Price sat around straight on the bench. "So you think we should all be on the lookout?"

"I should say so. It may not seem like much to the average cowpuncher, and I know a lot of 'em don't want to tell on someone else. But it's what butters your bread. Let these thieves have their way, and there won't be a ranch left to pay wages." Overlin had a glare in his eyes. "It's not easy to build a ranch and try to hold it together, and then these no-goods come along. Rather steal than work. Pilfer any way they can. Tear down what other people build up."

Silence set in again. Rucker appeared at the kitchen doorway, a short, slender man with a shiny bald head, short brown hair, and a clipped mustache. He wiped his hands on his apron.

"What do you want?" Overlin asked.

"Nothin'. I just came to see what was goin' on."

"Well, it's all for now. I've said enough. We'll see more about it as we go along." Overlin gave his pipe a light rap on the ashtray, rose from his seat, and took his hat from the peg. "Good night, boys. See you in the morning."

The bunkhouse door was open to let out the heat of the cook-stove and the smoke of fried bacon when Overlin returned in the morning. He was wearing his brown hat, with its peaked crown and four dents, and he did not take it off as he stood inside the doorway. In some light, as at the moment, the hat had a greenish tint. It did not look out of place with the boss's dark blue jacket and matching pants. As he often did when he went riding, Overlin carried a gun in a brown holster, which was visible beneath the open jacket. He was also wearing spurs on his dark brown boots.

Having made his appearance and gathered the attention of the four hired hands at the table, he said, "Boys, we're going to ride out together this morning. Jim, saddle the dun for me. He didn't work very hard yesterday, and he could use a little more exercise."

Price nodded. "You bet."

"I'm going back to the house. Let's be ready in about fifteen minutes." The boss walked out through the open door and left the men to finish their breakfast.

Del picked out a bay horse for the day's ride and tied him in front of the barn in the morning light. He took his time to brush the horse, comb its black mane and tail, and look at its hooves. He spoke to the animal as he laid on the blanket and pad and swung the saddle into place. He cinched up, traded the halter for a bridle, and led the horse out into an area clear of everyone else. He checked the cinch, tightened it another notch, and waited.

Macmillan and Westfall stood by with their mounts ready as Price worked on his own horse. The boss's zebra dun was tied by a neck rope to the hitching rail, ready to go.

Price finished rigging his horse, led it out, and handed the reins to Westfall. He returned to the hitching rail, untied the dun, and led it by the reins to a foot-high wooden step that served as a mounting block. He set the reins in place and held the horse by the headstall, near the bit, as Overlin came out of the house, stepped up onto the block, and mounted the horse.

Del put his foot in the stirrup and swung aboard. As he reined the bay around, he saw that Macmillan and Westfall were ready to go as well. Price led his horse aside, swung up onto it in a smooth motion, and waited for Overlin to take the lead.

Price rode alongside the boss as the group headed north out of the ranch yard. Del and Macmillan rode next, and Westfall took up the rear. The horse he rode was an old sorrel that hung its head, and Westfall had a drooping expression to match. The pair reminded Del of old illustrations he had seen in storybooks. This one could be of a lone traveler in a valley of sorrow.

The horse hooves clip-clopped, saddle leather creaked, and the animals heaved and snorted. Del wondered about the nature of the day's errand, but Overlin was like other bosses he had known, who did not inform the hired men any more or any sooner than necessary. Del figured he would find out soon enough.

The group paused at Coldwater Creek where it curved around to the north after flowing out of Coldwater Canyon and before straightening out to run east. Like many creeks in the region, it had grassy banks and a muddy bottom. It ran through public land, so it was not a formal dividing line, and cattle had no sense of boundaries in the absence of a fence. Nevertheless, as Del pulled the bay's muzzle out of the water and spurred the animal across the stream, he had a sense of leaving the larger cattle outfits behind and crossing over into the land of smaller homestead claims. With the sun at his back, he felt the sweat trickle beneath his shirt. He wondered again where they were headed and how long the day's ride would be.

A couple of miles farther, but still before any nester claims came into view, Overlin spoke to Price, and the horses began to veer left.

"Someone up there," said Macmillan.

Del nudged his horse to drift out of line to the right so he could see. A quarter mile ahead, three men sat on horseback. Del recognized Rich Hardesty and his man Fisher, but he did not know the third man.

The five riders from the Spoke came to a stop for about a minute, long enough for Del to hear the stranger's name, Lee Hilton, and to catch a glimpse of him.

The man had the general appearance of being from somewhere else. He had tapadero stirrups and a flat-crowned, flat-brimmed, dusty black hat. His face had the deeper tan of southern deserts, and he wore a cotton jacket with brown and yellow stripes. He had a lean face, a short, dark beard, and beady eyes. As the riders milled and fell into their new positions, Del saw that Hilton did not carry a rope or wear spurs. He wore lightweight leather riding gloves, and he was opening and closing his hands.

Overlin and Hardesty led the way, followed by Hilton and Fisher, then Del and Macmillan. Price took his place at the end, next to Westfall, with a half-smile on his face and a toothpick in the corner of his mouth.

As the day grew warmer, and with three additional horses, the group raised more dust than before, along with bits of dead grass. The soil was lighter here, and the horse hooves fell with duller sounds. Del felt the dry matter stick to his face, which had the dampness of perspiration but was not yet dripping with sweat.

From his shadow, Del guessed the time of day to be between ten-thirty and eleven. The sun beat down, and no breeze stirred. The flies became more persistent.

Word came relayed from the front as Hardesty's man Fisher spoke over his shoulder. "Fan out one on each side and stay close together."

Still not sure of their purpose, Del found himself angling to the right. As he came around, a scene came into view. A man stood on the ground near a speckled horse with a plain brown saddle. He had one hand on a rope tied to the saddle horn, and with the other hand he was slipping the loop off a calf's neck. The calf jumped up and ran away. The man coiled the rope as he moved backward toward his horse.

The men on horseback formed an arc facing the man on foot, and the group came to a stop. Price took up the far right, then Del, and then Macmillan. Overlin and Hardesty occupied the center, followed by Hilton, Fisher, and then Westfall, who had been directed to place himself on the far left. *Eight to one,* Del thought.

The man standing on the ground moved his head back and forth, as if he, too, was counting. He was not very tall, but he had a tough, unflinching look about him. He was dark-haired with a full mustache, thick eyebrows, and dark, searching eyes. He wore a light-colored, flat-brimmed hat with a low, round crown, matched in color by a full-buttoned shirt with chest pockets. A faded blue bandana hung around his neck, and a white-handled pistol rode on his hip.

Overlin spoke. "Tell us your name."

"You know my name as well as anyone does."

"Not everyone here does."

"It's Holt Warren. Now what do you want?"

Overlin's voice came out loud and clear. "We want to see the law obeyed. What are you doing here?"

Warren waved his hand. "Ah, go on. This is free range. I've got a right to be here just as much as anyone does."

Overlin cleared his throat. "What I mean is, what were you doing with your rope on that calf?"

Warren frowned. "Takin' a sticker out of its eye. It's my calf, got my brand on it." He crossed in front of his horse, tied the rope to his saddle, and returned to stand in front of his horse with the reins in his left hand. His right hand hung near his pistol. "Now maybe I could ask you the same question. What are you doing here?"

Hardesty spoke. "Like Bill said, we're tryin' to get people to follow the law."

"Well, I am."

"Maybe right now."

Overlin cut in. "We've got reason to believe you've been branding stock, especially calves, outside of the auspices of the Wyoming Stock Growers Association."

Warren had his fists clenched at his sides now. "I've done nothin' of the sort."

Overlin continued to speak in a clear, deliberate tone. "Say what you want, but we've got good evidence that some branding has gone on between sanctioned roundups."

"And you brought your army here to tell me that?"

"Rules are rules."

"Hah. I know how well you've always followed principle."

Overlin's face stiffened, and his mouth moved without his speaking. He adjusted the reins in his gloved hands and said, "Watch what you say."

Warren's eyebrows went up. "Too close to the truth, huh? And with your men present to hear it."

Overlin made a small spitting sound, as if he had a fleck of tobacco to get rid of. "I'm telling you what we came here for. We've got a complaint against you."

"Written?"

"No. Spoken."

Warren waved his hand. "Ah, go to hell. You're full of—" Movement caused him to look to his right.

Lee Hilton swung down from his horse and flung the reins behind him. He had taken off his gloves and striped jacket at some point, and his lean figure bent forward in a close-fitting, collarless shirt with three buttons. He had a wide gun belt with cartridges, and a six-gun with a dark wooden handle rode in a holster. He flexed his hands, which did not look sun-tanned or work-hardened. He came to a stop, pulled himself up with a sniffing breath, and fixed his beady eyes on Holt Warren. He said, "Watch your tongue, mister, or I'll cut it out."

Warren looked him over. "What do you have to do with this?"

"As much as I want. You were on the verge of calling someone a liar."

Warren moistened his lips as he kept his eyes steady on Hilton. "Somebody went past the verge of telling me I broke the law when I didn't."

"And so you call him a liar."

"If something's not true, I say so." Warren frowned. "Who are you, anyway?"

"I work for the Pyramid. And my boss says you've been brandin' calves against the law. Do you want to call him a liar?"

"I'll say it's not true, no matter who says it."

"What if I do?"

The world went silent, and time stood still.

Warren said, "Mister, I don't know what your game is. Or why it takes eight men to gang up on me."

Hilton's voice was slow and menacing. "Get this. I don't need anyone else. I can take care of you by myself. You're just a tit-suckin', whimperin' calf rustler, never had a nickel to your name, never had a woman that would look at you, never had the guts to stand up for yourself, never—"

Holt Warren's hand dropped to the ivory-handled pistol at his side, and then it seemed as if he thought better of it, but he had gone too far.

Lee Hilton had drawn his dark-handled six-gun, quick as a snake, and he placed one shot in the middle of Holt Warren's greyish-white shirt. A red spot appeared as Warren stepped back, clutched his abdomen, and fell to the side.

John D. Nesbitt

His speckled horse, with its grey and yellow mane flying, galloped away. The animal held its head to one side as the stirrups flopped and the reins trailed.

Chapter Two

Holt Warren's horse was standing in the corral when Del went out to saddle a mount for the day's work. The animal was not wearing a saddle. Its speckles were faint in the morning light, and the grey and yellow mane gave it a ghostlike appearance. Del did not want to go near it or be implicated in any way. He stood still for a moment, rope in hand. Westfall appeared at his elbow and spoke as if he had his teeth clenched.

"Hardesty and Fisher brought this thing by in the middle of the night. I couldn't sleep after what happened yesterday, and I was sitting outside in the moonlight, so I saw 'em."

"Does the boss know?"

"I believe so. They stopped at the house."

Del tried to make sense of the situation. The evening before, he understood that Overlin had gone with Hardesty and the two Pyramid men to deliver the body and report the incident. They could provide a handful of witnesses who, whether they liked it or not, would have to confirm that Holt Warren had gone for his gun first. Now his horse was here, of all places. Del reasoned that the Pyramid men must have found the horse on or near their range, and Hardesty must have thought that Overlin would have a good way of turning it over to the right people. The Pyramid could stay out of the way, and Overlin could give the impression that he was doing things right. Still, it seemed strange, and Del hoped he did not have to take part in it.

Back to the task at hand, Del picked out a sorrel from his

string and took it out in front of the barn to work on it. Macmillan showed up with a dark horse that had a white star on its forehead. He tied up near Del and went to work. Price and Westfall were saddling their horses in the barn. Del preferred to take his horse outside when the weather permitted, to avoid crowding and mishaps. He didn't mind carrying his saddle and bridle, and the better light helped him see any nicks or sores on the animal. Macmillan often saddled up inside, so Del thought his fellow puncher had taken his horse outside because he wanted to share a comment.

Del was pulling a steel comb through the sorrel's tail when footsteps sounded. He finished combing and stood by the horse's hip as the boss approached. Macmillan kept brushing until Overlin came to a stop and spoke.

"Boys, I've got an errand for the two of you." After a pause, as if to be sure he had their attention, he said, "You may have seen that other horse in the corral. It showed up here last night. Someone needs to take it where it belongs. Mac, you know where the fellow's place is, don't you?"

"Yes, but I believe he lived alone."

"I think you're right. So if you don't find anyone there, take it to one of his neighbors. There should be someone out there to take care of things by now, but they may have come and gone. We don't want to just leave the horse there. We want people to know that we made sure it got back into the right hands."

Del had to keep himself from staring. Even though he had already guessed at the motive, he was taken aback by the boss's pretense that no one had done anything wrong and that he was doing things right.

Macmillan said, "We'll see to it."

"The saddle's in the barn. Make sure it goes, too, of course."

★ ★ ★ ★ ★

Del let out a long breath as he and Macmillan put the first hill behind them. They were headed in the same direction as the morning before, but instead of riding along with a sense of light curiosity, he felt the pressure of being pushed by something he did not agree with but could not call by name.

He spoke to Macmillan. "Could you believe the way he said what he did?"

"I know what you mean. Barefaced. He sets it up to have a man killed, and then he acts as if he's lookin' out for the man's property. He drags us into it yesterday, then makes us do the dirty work today." Macmillan glanced back at the speckled horse on the end of the lead rope. "I wanted to ask him why the Pyramid boys didn't take this horse back, since they were closer to begin with, but of course I didn't. Sometimes I think he doesn't like me anyway. Then again, sometimes I think he doesn't like anyone."

"All of this is strange. None of us Spoke riders did a thing. That fellow Hilton did the shootin', but like you say, we all got dragged into it. And now here we are, tryin' to put a good face on it."

"It's queer. You know they had it set up with that newcomer Hilton. How would he have known what to say otherwise? And all this because someone's got a suspicion that someone is rustlin' stock. And even that seems flimsy to me."

Del shook his head. "I didn't know the fella, but he didn't seem all that bad to me. I imagine he had friends. I wonder what kind of a hostile reception we might be riding into."

"We're just doin' our job."

"Yeah, I know."

Macmillan led the way along a dusty trail to a set of weathered buildings in the middle of a quarter-section parcel of grassland.

"This is Warren's place," he said. "He's got it fenced. I thought homesteaders were supposed to plant a certain amount of land, but I don't see where he ever did. As far as I know, he always ran cattle."

No signs of life appeared as they rode into the yard. The sun of late morning heated the bare ground, and the sparse weeds had dried up and gone to seed. On the left side of the yard, a stable with its roof slanting to the west stood with its door open. Farther back and in the middle, a smaller outbuilding had its roof slanting the same way. On the right side of the yard, facing the approach from the south, stood the house. It was a bit larger than a homesteader's shack, about twenty feet by twenty-four, with a small front porch and overhang. To the left side of the door, an old singletree hung from a nail. The right side was lower than the left, like an uneven scale with no trays.

Macmillan called out, "Anyone home?" After a moment of silence, he said, "I guess we go on to the next place."

They rode east for about a mile until they came to a parcel that showed signs of having been plowed up. A couple of patches had gone to weeds, but a larger portion of about twenty acres, fenced, had the gleam of wheat stubble. Del recalled that wheat harvest had gone on about a month earlier. South of the wheat field, a green garden patch sat on the west side of a whitewashed house and barn.

Macmillan led the way around to the front of the house. Del expected a barking dog to appear, but only a couple of chickens cackled. The front door opened.

An older man with his girth covered in bib overalls stepped out into the shade of the porch. He had light-colored hair running to grey, a curly beard to match, and a full face with a rosy tint. His eyes went back and forth. "What can I do for you fellas?"

Macmillan said, "We're lookin' for friends of Holt Warren. We have a horse of his to deliver."

The man on the porch squinted. "Is that right? And who are you boys?"

"We ride for the Spoke brand. Bill Overlin's outfit. He said the horse showed up at the ranch, and he sent us over with it."

"I imagine he knows what happened. Wasn't he there?"

"Yes, he was. But it was a man from the Pyramid that fired the shot."

"So we heard. And now you're lookin' for Holt's friends?"

"At least one."

"It so happens that there's more than one of 'em here. Neighbors, at least. We're havin' coffee. Why don't you come in out of the sun and say what you have to say to all of 'em?"

Del wondered how big of a group waited inside. For all he knew, there might be a vigilante group forming. He glanced at Macmillan, who shrugged and said, "I suppose it's all right."

The riders swung down and tied the three horses at the rail.

The man in the overalls waited by the door as they stepped up onto the porch. "My name's Branch Wiggins," he said.

Closer, Del saw that the man had a clear complexion, not very tanned, and quick blue eyes. Del shook his hand, which was pale and soft.

Inside the house, two men sat at a table with tan crockery coffee mugs in front of them. They both looked like farmers, one in middle age and one about thirty.

On the wall in back of the older man hung an illustration in black and white. It featured a woman wearing a full dress with a high collar and long sleeves. She had her hair pinned up, and her facial features had an earnest cast to them. She was seated on a simple wooden armchair with a cherub of a girl in her lap, a boy sitting on the floor next to her foot, and a dog next to the boy. The caption read "The Angel in the House," which Del recognized as the title of a long, sentimental poem about the ideal devoted wife.

Del brought his awareness back to the moment at hand. He and Macmillan took off their hats and remained standing as Wiggins took a seat at the table.

"Tell us your name, boys."

"I'm Oswald Macmillan, and this here is Del Rowland. We ride for the Spoke brand, owned by Bill Overlin."

"So you said. Well, you know my name." Wiggins tipped his hand toward the middle-aged man on his right. "This is my neighbor, Homer Templeton. He farms on his own, and he leases some of my land."

Templeton spoke in a deep voice. "Pleased t'meet ya." He was a slender man with straight dark hair, jug ears, a rough complexion, and a prominent Adam's apple. He wore a coarse grey work shirt with brown suspenders, and his large hands worked at one another.

"And this here's another neighbor, George Clede. He has his own place and works out as well."

Del and Macmillan both nodded, as they did with Templeton. Clede did not speak at first but raised his chin and gave them both a looking-over. He had long, straight, light-colored hair, a narrow face, close-set dark eyes, a spindle nose, and a thin mouth. He was small-chested, but he had a rounded back and shoulders, which reminded Del of men he had seen who spent a great part of their lives humping sacks of grain. Pointed teeth showed as he said, "Hullo."

Wiggins spoke again. "Tell us why you're here, boys."

Macmillan turned to Del. "Your turn."

Del cleared his throat. "Well, our boss sent us over here with Holt Warren's horse. He said it showed up at the ranch, and he wanted to be sure it ended up in the right hands."

"Too bad about what happened," said Templeton in his deep voice.

"Poor Holt," said Wiggins. "He won't see new green grass again."

Del glanced at Clede, who kept his mouth closed in a sullen expression.

Wiggins continued. "Not that any of us think he would brand cattle that weren't his own, and I can't blame him for resenting an accusation. But he was a little quick to temper. And the way the story came to us, he went for his gun first. Is that right?"

Del took a breath. "I'm sorry to say it, but that's what happened."

Clede's teeth showed. "So you were there? And you come by now, makin' up?"

Macmillan spoke. "Two things here. For one, none of us boys that ride for the Spoke did a thing. We were just there. The fella who did the shootin' works for the Pyramid, and his name's Hilton. Second, we came over here because that was our job today. We've got no ill will toward anyone."

Wiggins tipped his head back and forth. "No one wants trouble. We've got our own interests to look after, and none of us is going to fight about branding cattle. And as for you boys doin' your job, that seems all on the square with me."

"Thanks," said Macmillan. "Can we leave the horse here, then?"

"You can put it in the barn and come back in. I want you boys to sit down and have a cup of coffee. Matter of fact, it only takes one of you to do that." He nodded to Macmillan, then said to Del, "Have a seat."

As Macmillan walked away and Del laid his hand on an empty chair, Wiggins shouted over his shoulder, "Tess!"

Del would not have imagined there was another person in the house, but it made sense that Wiggins would be so free with his hospitality if someone else was doing the work. Assuming that Tess was the name of Mrs. Wiggins, Del expected to hear the heavy tread of a woman to match the man in overalls. He waited, imagining an indistinct form advancing with a coffeepot at apron level.

A female form appeared in an instant, it seemed, passing through the doorway with a brisk step. A young woman of middle height, with dark hair and shining eyes, took in the room with a glance. She was wearing a grey apron and a dark blue dress. She came to a stop, wiping her hands on a dishcloth and settling her eyes on Wiggins. "Yes?"

"We've got more company. This young fella and his partner who's puttin' a horse in the barn. I offered 'em a cup of coffee."

"I believe there's enough in the pot." Tess gave a tip of the head to the group, took half a step backward, and turned away.

"My niece," said Wiggins. "She helps with the farmyard work as well as the housework."

Del nodded in recognition to the uncle.

Clede had his lower lip pushed against the upper as he stared at his coffee cup. Templeton was working his hands as before, as if they wanted to be handling the reins of a plow horse.

From Clede's expression, Del sensed something like jealousy or resentment. A couple of minutes earlier, Del had thought that Wiggins had made the invitation in order to stay on good terms with the big cattleman's men, but now it seemed as if the uncle might have a sense of courtesy or obligation to introduce young people to one another. That thought, in turn, suggested that the uncle did not consider Clede to be the suitor that he, Clede, would like to be or thought he should be.

Tess returned with a blue enamel coffeepot and two more tan cups. As she poured the coffee, Del noticed a small red ribbon and bow where she had her hair pinned up. When she turned her head and smiled, he saw that her lips were red as well.

"More?" she asked, looking around.

Clede said, "I'll take some."

Templeton pushed his hands flat in the direction of his cup. "None for me, thanks. I need to get back to my place and do some work." He scraped the floor as he moved his chair back.

Wiggins said, "It was good that you could come by. I'll go to the door with you." He shifted his chair to one side and pushed himself to his feet. After straightening up and taking a breath, he followed Templeton out onto the porch and closed the door behind him.

Del surmised that the neighbors had come over to talk about the Holt Warren incident and that Wiggins wanted to close the conversation with Templeton. Clede, on the other hand, showed no inclination to budge.

Tess had set the coffeepot on the table and stood now with her hands folded.

"I'm sorry," said Del. "We haven't been introduced. My name is Del Rowland. I work for a cattle outfit south of here. The Spoke. My riding partner should be here in a minute or two."

"My name is Tess Lang. I think my uncle told you I help him out."

"He did."

"I'm a country girl to begin with. I grew up on my parents' farm, so it's all familiar to me."

"That's good."

Clede spoke up. "He was with the bunch that had the skirmish yesterday. He works for one of the big outfits."

Del held his teeth together for a second, then spoke. "As my partner and I told these men, we didn't have a hand in it. We came here today to deliver Holt Warren's horse, to make sure it ended up in the right hands."

Clede said, "He wants to take credit for the good part."

Tess had a cross tone in her voice as she said, "Why don't you let him say what he wants?" She turned her dark eyes to Del. "Go ahead."

Del took a second so as not to hurry his words. "As for bring-ing the horse back, that wasn't our idea, either. We were sent to do it. But once we're here, I want to do my job, which is to place this man's property with reliable people."

Clede gave a backward wave of the hand. "We don't care for meddlers, especially do-gooders who carry out orders for the mucky-mucks."

Tess took a more patient tone than before. "There's no need to be harsh with this man. He says he wants the horse to end up with the right people, and I don't see anything wrong with that."

"People say they want one thing, and then you find out they want something else."

Del spoke to Tess. "Thank you for giving me credit." He flickered a glance at Clede and returned to her. Her eyes gave him encouragement to say more. "If there's anything else that I want, it's not something material. Rather, and I hope I don't sound too blunt, what I want is to follow my conscience. If there was a way I could help set things right, I would do it."

Clede blurted, "But you're on their side."

Del took a breath to keep from giving an angry retort. "I work for a living, but I had no hand in this man's death, and I won't go along with anything crooked."

"That's easy to say."

Del did not want to give Clede the last word, but he did not want to contribute to a bad-natured argument, so he said, "We'll see." He sipped on his coffee and found it lukewarm.

Rising voices from outside suggested that Wiggins and Templeton were ending their conversation. A second exchange followed between Wiggins and what sounded like Macmillan. The door opened, and Wiggins shuffled in.

"I think your partner is impatient to go. I tried to get him to come in, but he says you need to be on your way."

"I suppose I'd better not keep him waiting." Del drank half of his remaining coffee and set the cup down. He met Tess's eyes again and said, "Thank you."

She smiled. "You're welcome."

As he rose from his chair, he cast a glance at Clede and said, "Good to meet you."

"Likewise."

Del paused at the door for a soft handshake with his host. "Thank you, Mr. Wiggins, and I look forward to seeing you again."

"Ha-ha. I've never gotten used to people callin' me Mister."

"I don't know you that well."

"Well, no, you don't. It's not like Tess when she was little. She called me Nuncle Wiggie." He chortled. "Cutest little thing. You'd never know it now. Ha-ha."

Del turned toward Tess, and he made himself meet her eyes and not look at the rest of her. She was anything but homely. From her glance, he understood that she tolerated her uncle's humor. He also interpreted that the uncle was proud to have an attractive niece in a country where women were scarce. With his hat still in his hand, Del said, "Very well. Until next time."

Out on the trail, Del said to Macmillan, "I didn't know you were in a hurry."

"I didn't see any reason to loiter. I've met Clede before, and I don't care for him. Besides, I thought if we used our time well, we could stop in town."

Del pictured the detour. "Not a bad idea in itself. But I think it's only fair to tell you that you missed out on meeting Uncle Wiggie's niece."

"Oh, go on. The only other person in there was that sourpuss Clede."

"Think what you want, but her name's Tess. I wouldn't force you to meet her. Clede is enough of a rival himself."

"You're kidding."

"Not about the girl. She's real enough. As for Clede, at least he sees himself as a contender. If he was any more, I doubt that Wiggins would have wanted us to meet her."

"Just my luck. Maybe next time."

Del and Macmillan were tying their horses in front of the Forge Saloon when a drumming of hooves and a rattling of gear announced the arrival of a stagecoach. A few seconds later, a team of four horses pulled into view and came to a stop in a cloud of dust that drifted on. The wheels and undercarriage of the vehicle were painted yellow, and the body was a deep brown. Passengers' heads were visible. The driver called out, "Provenance. Five minutes."

A small crowd gathered as six passengers, all men, stepped down and began walking around. One of them lit a cigar and said, "Did he say Providence?"

"Provenance," said an onlooker. "That's where you are."

The driver tossed down a mail sack, but no one unloaded luggage or parcels. With no new arrivals to look at, Del and Macmillan made their way into the Forge Saloon.

The bar ran the length of the left side of the interior. Behind the bar, two dark, varnished pillars rose to a height of seven feet with a panel of mirrors between them. A little over halfway down the bar, two older men in town clothes stood talking. At the far end, the bartender was polishing a clear glass goblet with a white cloth. Beyond him, on the end wall, an anvil sat on a stout shelf with a hand sledge hanging on the wall above it.

The bartender set his work aside and walked along the bar to face his new patrons. He was an older man, past middle age, with grey hair, spectacles, sagging cheeks, and a neck like a turtle. Del recalled that his name was Mitchell.

"What'll it be?" the man asked.

Macmillan said, "How cold is your beer, Mitch?"

"As cold as you're going to find in this town."

"Then we'll take two. One each."

Mitchell served the two glasses and stepped back, rubbing his hands on his apron. "You work for the outfit that took part in the shootin' yesterday, don't you?"

Macmillan answered. "Yes, we do."

"I thought you did." The bartender walked back to the end of the bar and took up his white cloth.

Del took a drink from his glass. The beer was not cold, but it was not warm, either. He took another sip and resumed taking stock of his surroundings.

Macmillan stood at Del's right, and the two older men stood five or six feet down the bar. Del could see them in the mirror. The nearer one had straight white hair, thinning on top, and wore a light tan suit with a white shirt. Del had seen him before but did not remember his name.

After a couple of minutes, the man moved closer to Macmillan. "You work for Bill Overlin."

"That's right."

"We've met before. My name's Norris Drayton."

"You're a dentist."

"I was for many years. Retired now. Who's your friend?"

"Del Rowland."

Drayton leaned forward on the bar, looked past Macmillan, and said, "Pleased to meet you."

Del leaned forward and saw the man's blue eyes and narrow nose, which was red on the sides. "Pleasure's mine."

Drayton settled back to speak to Macmillan again. "We were sorry to hear about what happened yesterday. I hope you don't mind my asking, but were you there?"

"Yes, we were, but none of us from the Spoke had any idea of what anyone had in mind, and none of us had a hand in what happened."

"That's what we heard. Your outfit was there, but a man from the Pyramid did the shooting."

Drayton's friend took his place next to the old dentist, away from the bar, and handed him his drink. Del stepped around to form a foursome.

"Talkin' about the killin?" said the other man. "Terrible thing."

"This is Josh Crittenden," Drayton said.

Del and Macmillan gave their names.

Drayton said, "These boys say they were there but didn't have anything to do with it."

"Well, it's no good," said Crittenden. He was a common-looking man, of average height, with light brown hair and a mustache, both greying, along with glasses and an aging face. He held a whiskey glass and rocked on his feet. He took a small sip, pursed his mouth, and relaxed it, though it was still wrinkled.

Drayton set his drink on the bar and took a cigarette case from his coat pocket. He opened it and showed two rows of rolled cigarettes in tan paper. To Del, they looked like the kind that a person rolled himself, ten or twenty at a time, with a small manual machine. Drayton offered the case to the two cowpunchers, who both declined. He did not bother to offer it to his friend. He took out a cigarette for himself, found a match, and lit up. He blew out a long stream of smoke and turned his tired eyes to settle on the two young men.

"I'll make no secret of it," he began. "Holt Warren was a friend of ours. I don't think you boys'll bear me a grudge if I stick up for him."

The boys shook their heads.

"Well, to begin with, I don't think he would brand any cattle that weren't his. I think he knew how to stay out of trouble, so I doubt he would have done any branding out of season, though a man ought to have a right to brand his own stock in his own corral. Spoken as a private citizen. I know the Association doesn't see things that way. But they've always had a high-and-mighty attitude, like might makes right. And Holt knew they were looking for scapegoats, someone to pick on. His only shortcoming was that he had contempt for them."

Del said, "Because of the attitude you mention?"

"That, among other things." Drayton took a drink. "Some of these big cattlemen act as if they were here first and should have the authority to keep their old ways. They treat nesters like newcomers that are tryin' to break down the order. But that's really not the case. Most of these nesters have been here quite a while, and they came on legal terms set by the government. Meanwhile, the cattlemen think they should get away with doing things like they did twenty years ago, when the Stock Growers Association had even more power than it does now." Drayton raised his eyebrow, shrugged, and took another drag on his cigarette.

Del realized that Drayton had come around to where he had started, restating the might-makes-right attitude. He wondered what "other things" might have given Holt Warren cause for contempt, but he sensed that Drayton had said as much on that subject as he cared to say for the time being.

"How long were you a dentist?" Del asked.

"It seemed like all my life, but it was only thirty-four years. Now that's all in the past, and I'm just tryin' to make things last. You're young, and you don't want to hear all this. But I'll tell you, we all get one chance, and we all use it differently."

Macmillan said, "Do you ever wish you were still working?"

"Not very much."

Macmillan raised his chin toward Crittenden. "How about you?"

"Oh, I'm still working. This is just my dinner hour. I go back to work at two."

"Damn me. I lose track of time in these places."

Drayton gave a short laugh. "Wait till you get older."

"I'm in no hurry for that. But I did remember that we have to get back to the ranch." Macmillan tipped up his glass.

Del did the same. "I'm ready when you are."

CHAPTER THREE

When Bill Overlin came to the bunkhouse the next morning, he was not wearing a pistol or spurs. He hung his hat on a peg and sat down at the table, where the hired men were eating hotcakes. Rucker poured him a cup of coffee. The boss showed no hurry at all as he touched his coffee cup with his right hand and stared at the table. He was clean-shaven as usual, and though his lower eyelids were full and his face carried a bit of flesh, he had the appearance of a man who ate well and slept well and did not have to worry about the rent and the grocery bill.

Utensils clacked on plates as the men put away the food. Westfall was the first to finish. He pushed his plate back, moved his coffee cup closer, and began to roll a cigarette.

The boss had an absent gaze until Westfall lit the cigarette. A faint scowl passed over his face. He tucked his head back and took a drink of coffee. As he set his cup down, he spoke in Price's direction.

"Jim, you and Ed ride out as usual. Keep your eyes open for anything that looks out of place. You know what I think, and I want to know about anything that's going on."

"You bet."

The boss shifted in his seat. "Mac, I'll have you ride out on your own today. Same orders. Let me know if you see anything."

"I will."

"Del, my wife has a job for you. Knock at the back door, and she'll tell you what she wants."

"Yes, sir."

Overlin pressed the tips of both hands on the table. "That should be good for right now. I'm going back to the house. I'll be tied up with bookwork and figures."

Del reached for his coffee cup. As a general rule, the boss did not announce to his men what he was going to be doing. Del thought it might be another way of saying that he would be counting losses.

Del took off his hat as he knocked at the back door of the ranch house. Footsteps sounded, and the door opened to reveal Diana Overlin. Del had not seen her up close before. When he had seen her around the yard, she was covered up with a shawl or a mantle and wore a wide straw hat tied on with a scarf, but she always looked like a woman who kept her figure up. She looked no less so now, in a full dress with a buttoned collar, all in pale yellow, with a pair of clean grey cotton gloves. Her blond hair was pinned up, and she wore small, tiger-eye earrings. She had a very smooth complexion, almost perfect, which Del imagined was the result of applying creams and lotions and staying out of the sun and wind. Her blue eyes had a soft shine, and she gave a polite smile.

"Thank you for coming. Bill said he would send someone."

Del nodded.

"I'll tell you what I need. We're into the latter part of August, and the chokecherries are ripening. I would like to have a few before the birds get them all."

"Yes, ma'am."

She reached down to her left, and with her gloved hand she lifted two three-gallon tin pails. "Not much. Just enough to make a little jelly."

Del caught the scent of aromatic powder as he took the pails by the handles. "These don't fill up very fast, but I'll do the best I can."

"I'm sure you'll do fine. And thank you."

"Glad to do it." Del put on his hat as she closed the door. He had picked chokecherries before, and he knew it would take the better part of the morning to fill the two buckets.

After stopping at the bunkhouse to take off his spurs, he walked to the southwest, past the edge of the ranch yard, to a gully where a thicket of chokecherry bushes grew. Half a dozen birds flew out of the foliage as he approached.

The fruit looked black and juicy as it hung among the dark green leaves, but as soon as he picked the first handful, he recalled that it was red as well. The pea-sized, hard little cherries pinged as they hit the inside of the pail. He worked for several minutes, holding the branch with one hand and stripping with the other, and the bottom of the pail was still not covered. His hands were sticky, and he had to pick out leaves, stems, twigs, and bits of old, dead blossoms. At the top of a branch, he found some larger, darker fruit, and he popped a few into his mouth. As always, they had large pits for their size, with very little flesh or juice. His mouth puckered. He spit out the pits and continued working.

After an hour, he had about a quarter of a pail. The fruit was falling onto fruit, soft and quiet, in a dark mass. The sun was shining through the top leaves. No sounds came from the ranch yard. The Overlins did not keep chickens or other fowl, and the horses were all out to pasture for the day. Del was startled, then, when he heard a voice.

"Hey, puncher. They've got you working hard, it looks like."

Del let the branch flip up as he dropped a small handful of cherries into the pail. "I don't know if it's what I do best." He raised his eyes to see Lawna, looking fresh in a light tan dress with a placket down the middle and bows on the shoulders.

She said, "It looks like you're doing swell."

"I think I'm supposed to fill both of these buckets. It doesn't go very fast."

She smiled. "It doesn't make much jelly, either. But that's what gives value to some things—the amount of labor that goes into it. Don't look surprised. I didn't come up with that idea myself. I heard it from my mother, and I imagine she heard it from someone else."

"I'm sure it has some truth."

"Oh, yes. Think of all the things people do in the small, old way, while the rest of the modern world is inventing more and more labor-saving machines."

"A pleasant thought."

"I believe it applies to servants polishing silver, as well."

"I don't like to think of how well suited I would be for that. Maybe too well."

"Don't worry." She took a breath, as was her habit, and her bosom rose. "We don't have silver. My mother will have me stirring these with a wooden spoon, in a big kettle on a hot stove."

"Part of the value of the product." He decided he had better keep working, so he resumed picking.

"That, and it's part of my training for when I have a household of my own."

"I see."

"They want us all to go into harness."

He understood "they" to mean society in general as well as perhaps her parents. He tipped his head back and pulled down a branch. "Uh-huh. Is that very close on the horizon?"

"Not so much. No hurry on my part, that's for sure."

"Men are different."

"Oh, he's all right. He's not the only pebble on the beach, but we're a long ways from the ocean. And they keep telling me I'm not going to do any better out here."

42

"By 'they,' you mean your . . . family?" Del was glad to hit on the right word.

"Yes. My mother and my stepfather."

He thought it was easier not to be looking at her when she spoke in such a direct way. "Well, they have their ideas."

"Oh, yes."

He turned to pour the precious fruit from his cupped hands into the pail. He found her standing a couple of steps closer. As he straightened up, he noticed a pendant on her chest, a small garnet the size of a chokecherry stone. At the same time, he caught a dry, perfume-like aroma. He met her eyes and smiled. "You seem to do all right at thinking for yourself."

She smiled in a playful way. "Sometimes."

"Well, like you say, these are modern times."

"Yes. You'll know it when you see me smoking a cigarette in a long cigarette holder."

"I haven't seen that."

"It's new. I saw in a magazine that it's going to be a fashion."

"How does it go with holding the wooden spoon at arm's length?"

"I don't have them in the same picture."

He raised his eyebrows and returned to his work of picking fruit. He pulled down another branch and wrapped his hand around a small bunch.

Without any ceremony, she said, "Well, I guess I'll go back to the house."

"I didn't mean to turn my back on you."

"Oh, I know. I need to be going, anyway."

"Good enough. Nice of you to drop by and visit."

"It helps pass the time."

Del blinked his eyes at the sun as he let the branch go. He lowered the fruit to the pail. Lawna was walking toward the house at a medium pace, not in a stroll and not in a hurry. She

raised her hand in a wave. As she had her back to Del, he followed the motion.

Rich Hardesty had tied his horse in front of the barn and was
beginning to walk toward the ranch house.

Del raised his eyebrows. She must have seen him from a ways
out.

The sun had moved into midmorning, and Del had one full pail
of chokecherries sitting in the shade. He was pinging into the
second bucket when movement in the sunlight caught his eye.
Overlin was headed his way. Hardesty's horse was gone. The
boss did not have a determined stride, so Del did not feel a
cause for worry.

Overlin found a place to stand in the shade. "Slow work, isn't
it? I know that. Looks like you've got one bucket already. That's
better than some people. When Lawna was younger, she
wouldn't pick half that much in a whole day."

"It's all work."

"Yes, it is. And the man who doesn't think he's going to pick
his jobs will go farther." Del was holding the almost-empty pail
up to the branch and was stripping fruit into it. He paused to
pick out some leaves.

Overlin said, "I didn't get a chance to hear how things went
yesterday, over there with the nesters."

"Not much in particular. We left the horse with a man named
Wiggins."

"I know who he is."

"A couple of neighbors happened to be there, so from the
point of view of verifying how the horse was delivered,
everything was in plain view."

"That's good." Overlin paused for a few seconds. "What sorts
of things did they say?"

Del measured his words. "Oh, about what you could expect.

44

They said they didn't think he would do anything like change a brand, or brand someone else's stock, or even brand out of season."

"Of course they would say that. And you know damn well there's things goin' on night and day."

Del did not answer.

"Do you have a reason not to look at me when I'm talking to you?"

Del faced him. "No, sir. I just thought I should keep working."

The boss looked him over as if he was harmless, and he felt like a kid, standing there with juice stains on his hands and an almost-empty tin pail.

Overlin said, "I know what you mean. You want to keep at it if you ever hope to fill that thing." He gave a light wag of the head. "It makes good jelly, though, and when it doesn't jell, which is half the time or more, it makes good syrup. It would have gone well on those hotcakes this morning."

"I'm sure of that."

"Keep at it. You're doing all right." The boss took off his hat and wiped his brow with a white handkerchief as he walked away.

Del went back to picking the bead-like fruit. He reflected on the visit with Lawna, and he took cheer in thinking how much he was increasing the value of the jelly he would probably never see.

The sun continued to climb. Left to himself at his menial work, Del had the freedom of mind to reflect. He felt belittled by the interview with Overlin. The boss had talked down to him and had shown that he was sure of him. The boss assumed that if a man wanted a job, he would do what he was told. Conscience ate on Del as he recalled his conversation with Tess and Clede, when, at an easy moment, he said he wouldn't go along with anything crooked. And here he was, giving a straight face to what he was sure was a cooked-up theory about a rustling conspiracy. He felt as if he was living in an enclosed world, in which someone else was presuming to say what was real and what was not.

At the same time, he saw cracks in the shell. The nesters knew better, even though most of them were not going to volunteer information if there was any. Someone like Drayton, on the other hand, posed a greater likelihood of spilling some kind of beans. And closer to home, Lawna had shown an indication that she was not a blind loyalist. Del was convinced that something was crooked. By his own declaration, he should leave. But if he stayed a while longer, he might go away with information that would help the greater good. He just had to be careful. Even if the boss was sure of him, Overlin was no fool. He had come too far, and he had too much to protect.

Del counted the days. Tomorrow was Saturday. He and the other boys would ride into town in the evening. He could bide his time until then.

Del stood at the open back door of the bunkhouse and watched the rain come down. He had seen clouds building when he was out on his ride, and he had made it back to the barn in good time. Waiting now for his turn for a bath, he wondered if the rain would let up and allow the boys to go to town.

The sky thundered, and the rain fell. At first it brought the smell of moisture on dry earth, but that sensation passed as the rainfall became harder. Water was coming down in sheets and running across the ground in tiny floods, carrying debris and bits of brown foam. Heavy drops splashed as if they were jumping upward.

After twenty minutes, the rain slowed down. The clouds moved to the east, and the sun's reappearance cast a rainbow a few miles away with the clouds as background. Right outside, the air was fresh and clear, perfect for the tink-a-link song of a meadowlark.

Price appeared at his side. "What's it look like?"

"Clearing up. Looks like we'll get to go to town after all. Rained quite a bit in a short while, though."

Macmillan spoke from inside. "Summer rain. Before long we'll be getting the slow, cold rain. That's not any fun to go out into."

The meadowlark sang again. The world seemed clean as the late afternoon sunlight bathed the grassland that stretched away from the back door.

Del said, "We'll enjoy it while we can."

Piano music mingled with voices and laughter in the Forge Saloon. At least thirty men lined the bar and stood around in groups. Mitchell and a second bartender were wasting no time setting drinks on the bar and taking money. The first two girls in powder, paint, and feathers had made their appearance.

Del stood near the bar with Macmillan. Price and Westfall stood with a group of four or five others, all in their early twenties, who were taking turns making the others laugh. Del kept an eye out for riders from the Pyramid, but he did not see anyone familiar.

A light-colored figure made his way through the crowd. As he emerged, Del recognized the white-haired Norris Drayton. The older man was wearing a light grey suit with a white shirt and a grey striped vest. He moved with a jaunty gait, smiling and raising his hand in greeting. Del waved in return, and Drayton veered his way. As he came to a stop, his head swayed and settled into place. The suit he was wearing this evening showed a soft little belly and thin legs, and as he raised a tan cigarette to his lips, the lamplight fell on his yellow fingers.

"Evenin'. You're the young fella I met in here the other day, aren't you?"

"That's right. Del Rowland."

"I hope you made it back to work on time."

"We did. We had no trouble at all."

"That's good."

"Can I buy you a drink?"

"I wouldn't turn it down." The old dentist smiled and showed a good set of yellow teeth.

Del signaled to the bartender and pointed to Drayton. A minute later, the old man had a glass of whiskey to go with his cigarette. He seemed quite at ease in a crowd of younger, working men.

Macmillan, meanwhile, did not show as much interest in the man in the old suit as he did to a girl wearing a red, yellow, and white dress with a low neckline.

Drayton took a drink of whiskey. "You work for Bill Overlin."

Del said, "Yes, I do."

"I haven't seen Diana in a while. I suppose she looks as good as ever."

Del felt a pang of uneasiness at the mention of his boss's wife in a saloon. "Fine and healthy," he said.

"I knew her a long time ago. She was married to Paul Gresham, you know."

"I've heard the last name, but I'm not familiar with the history."

"Well, that was him. Had his own ranch out that way."

"I didn't know that."

The girl in the colored dress barged in. She brandished her charms to all three men as she spoke to Macmillan. "What are you up to this evening?"

Macmillan gazed at her. "Tryin' to stay out of trouble."

She batted her daubed eyelashes. "I don't blame you. There

are so many ways to fall into it."

Macmillan smiled. "But not with you."

She put her finger to her lip and shook her head in a slow, coy way. "Oh, no. Not with me. A boy stays out of trouble if he stays with me."

"That's what I thought. Get away from all this evil."

She moved close enough to brush against his arm. "That's right. Where it's nice and quiet."

Macmillan smiled again. "Let me finish my drink and think about it."

She laid her hand on his arm. "You can take your drink with you."

"I guess I can." Macmillan tipped a glance at Del. "I'll be back."

Del nodded. He tried to pay as little attention as possible, but he could not help notice how Price almost twisted his neck watching Macmillan go to the room.

Del returned to his friend of the moment. "Where were we?"

"I was telling you about Paul Gresham."

"Oh, yes."

"Had a ranch, a pretty wife, a little girl. What many a man dreams of. But he got caught in a snowstorm in Coldwater Canyon."

"I never knew that about the snowstorm. I knew Gresham was the girl's last name, though."

"It was a big story at the time."

"I can imagine."

"You asked the other day about Holt Warren."

Del wondered if the conversation had jumped a track. "We talked about him."

"He was part of the search party that found Paul and had to tell Diana."

"That must have been hard."

"You bet it was. He had been in love with her from the very beginning. But Paul had more going for him, and Holt took it like a man. Same thing when Paul died. Holt was full of respect, kept his distance."

"All very proper."

"Sure. And he watched Bill Overlin move right in."

Del's eyes went wide. "Onto the ranch?"

"No. He had his own ranch. The one he has now. He even had a wife before. Name of Imogene. She died that same bad winter. Complications from childbirth, couldn't get to town." Drayton held his cigarette sideways, stared at it, and sniffed.

"That sounds terrible. It must have been rough on everyone."

"Bill held up all right. He came out of it with two ranches and a lovely woman."

Del took a drink from his glass of beer.

"I'll tell you who it was rough on."

"Who?" Del expected him to say Lawna.

"Holt Warren."

Del felt as if had his breath taken away. He recalled Holt Warren's sarcastic comment about Overlin following principles, and he put it together with Drayton's comment about Warren having contempt for Overlin and others. He said, "I think I can understand why."

Drayton took a final drag on his cigarette, dropped the stub to the floor, and stepped on it. "I just mention it because you asked about him the other day."

"I guess I did."

Del and his older friend stood without speaking for a few minutes. The presence of a woman at Del's side caused him to turn. He expected to see one of the painted girls who had passed by earlier, but he saw a less gaudy version. She was still a woman of the night, but she had a more modest appearance, perhaps to go with her age. She was somewhere in the range between thirty-five and forty, with auburn-colored hair and hazel eyes. Her cheeks were beginning to sag, and she showed a little weight around the middle, but she had prominent peaks and what Del sensed as an inner glow. He felt a spark, or ripple, that he knew. With some voluptuous women, he could stand nearby and remain unmoved. With others, as with this woman, it was as if something from within spoke to something from within. Her eyes held him for a second, and she gave him a faint smile.

She spoke to Drayton. "How do you do, Norris? Have you been hiding this young man?"

"Not at all. And not from you. His name's Del, and he's an earnest lad. Del, this is my friend Maude." After a second, he added, "She's earnest, too."

Del tipped his hat. "Pleased to meet you."

She smiled as before. "And the same to you."

Drayton said, "Look who else is here."

Del took a step back to make room for a man who joined the group in an uneven motion, swinging his leg and settling himself on a dark cane. He had a singular appearance, as he wore a cap and a cloak. The cap was dark blue with a high front, like caps that went with various kinds of uniforms, but it did not have an insignia or a design on it. The cloak matched the cap in color, and the two items together looked as if they could have been borrowed from a palace guard or from the doorman of a hotel with a porte cochere.

The man was about forty years old, with grey showing in his hair and beard. His upper body looked healthy and muscled, but one leg was smaller than the other. The cane on which he steadied himself had an offset "T" handle, all in one piece, such as the kind that came from hard-grained fruit wood. When he was settled into place, he raised his chin and spoke to Drayton.

"I thought I would find you in a meeting of the old liars' club."

"Crittenden isn't here yet."

"I see that now. Good evening, Maude."

"Good evening, Malcolm. I see you're out spreading good-will."

"Like always." The man shifted the cane to his other hand, and with a hitch in his stance, offered to shake with Del. "Malcolm Bain."

Del reached forward and was met with a firm shake. "Del Rowland. Pleased to meet you."

"Likewise." The man adjusted his cane, took off his cap, and gave a light toss of the head. He had a full head of hair, mostly dark on top, that grew straight down on all sides and was trimmed across his forehead about an inch above his eyes. "Cowpuncher?"

"Yes."

"I'm an ostler."

"Oh."

Drayton said, "He works at the livery stable."

"I've heard the term before. I just wasn't sure."

Bain said, "I come in here, like a constable making the rounds, before I go on my shift." His face broke into a smile as he raised his head. "Well, lookee here. If it isn't my old pal."

Macmillan had returned from the room. "Well, what do you know! Malcolm Bain. Are you ready for a drink?"

"Just one. I'm on my way to work."

"I could sure use one." Macmillan put his arm around Bain's shoulders and ushered him to the bar.

Drayton smiled at Del. "We're all friends here."

"That's good." Del turned to Maude, and he was caught by her hazel eyes and restrained smile. He felt the ripple again, and her warm hand took his.

52

"We can be friends, too," she said as she raised her eyebrows. He felt a boldness. Motioning with his head toward the back door, he said, "There?"

"With me."

She gave a light pull, and he went with her. Price and the others watched him pass by, but he did not look at them. He saw the anvil on its shelf and the hammer on the wall, passed through a doorway, and followed the woman down a dim hall. She stopped, let go of his hand, and unlocked the door.

In the room, after taking his two dollars, she pointed to the side of the bed. "Sit here and take off your boots and the rest."

She went to the other side of the bed, and he heard her undress as he did the same. When he slipped under the covers, she was there to meet him.

The next several minutes were like a swirl and a dream as he went out of himself and into a world that was always there whenever he returned to it. Then it was over, and they had their backs to one another again, putting on their clothes.

He went back to the saloon by himself, after a short interlude, as Macmillan had done earlier and as Del had done in times past. He felt calm and restored, unbothered by the glances of the young men.

Malcolm Bain was nowhere in sight. Macmillan was talking with a couple of men from an outfit on Sheep Creek.

Del ordered a beer and joined Norris Drayton, who was standing by himself with his hands together holding a glass of whiskey and a tan cigarette with smoke curling up.

Del said, "You're giving me a funny look. Did I do something I shouldn't have?"

"Oh, no."

"She's not trouble, is she?"

Drayton shook his head. "Shouldn't be for you. There have been men who have gotten in trouble for knowing Maude, but that was because they were married."

"Well, I'm not, or anywhere near it."

"No harm in that." Drayton took a drag on his cigarette. "Nah, she's not all that bad. And she knew Holt Warren as well as anyone did."

Del's glance went to the back of the saloon, where the anvil and the hammer were mounted on the wall. Somewhere beyond, Maude was freshening up for her next client. He felt as if he had missed a chance to know more. Maybe he would see her again.

CHAPTER FOUR

Rucker was telling a story about raccoons from the time he was growing up in Nebraska. His family had chickens in cages that had wire screens for the floor, and the raccoons used to hang upside down from the wire and eat the toes off the chickens. Rucker's family used the new wire cages in order to keep the chickens up off the ground so their feet wouldn't cake up with mud and manure, especially in winter, and that was what they got for it.

Westfall, who did not talk much, said, "They're bad with turkeys, too. Turkeys are good to eat the grasshoppers, but if you've got turkeys, you'll have coons."

His eyes flickered to the doorway, and he flinched. There stood the boss, in his peaked hat and brown corduroy suit, fresh on Monday morning.

Rucker said, "That's for sure. And if you make a pet out of one, you'll never get rid of him. They make themselves at home. I had a friend who had a pet raccoon that would eat from his plate and take his tobacco from him. Playful-like. And then it bit his ear halfway off."

The boss walked in, and after an exchange of morning greetings, he began to assign the day's work. "Jim and Ed, I'll have you ride out south. Keep your eyes open as always. You never know where the trouble might be." Overlin shifted in his stance. "Mac and Del, I want you to ride north. Split up when you get to the other side of Coldwater Creek. I want you to get an idea of how much of my stock is on the north side of the creek. While you're at it, keep an eye out for anything that doesn't look right. I have a hunch I'm missing some cow-calf pairs, but it's hard to tell at this point." He let silence hang in the air for a couple of seconds. "You might want to take something to eat. I expect it'll take you the better part of the day."

When Del and Macmillan had the ranch headquarters well behind them, Del tossed out a casual question. "That area down south where the others are going today, it used to be the Gresham spread, didn't it?"

"At one time, from what I understand. Well before I came here."

"But no one lives there."

"No, there's no buildings. The way I heard it, there wasn't much built yet—just a house and a shed and some corrals. Bill had it all taken apart and brought up here. Lumber was expensive then, just like it is now, and it wasn't very old."

"And Coldwater Canyon ran along the west side of both ranches."

"That's right. Just like it does now, except it's all one ranch. The Spoke."

"I've heard it's a big canyon. I haven't been down in it myself. I worked the other side of that gather in the spring."

"It's deeper at the south end. It tapers down to almost nothin' where the creek flows out of it at the north end and then curves around."

"I know that end of it, of course."

Del placed the sun at about nine in the morning when they arrived at the creek and let the horses drink. He said, "Every time we cross this creek, it puts me in mind of that time about a week ago."

"I know what you mean."

"I had no idea we were going to meet up with those fellows from the Pyramid, much less what happened after that."

"Neither did I. It's an old story, but they still do things like that, and they still get away with it."

Del sensed that Macmillan was inclined to say something. Del said, "I've heard a little."

Macmillan went on. "First big instance of it was over on the Sweetwater. That was in 1889. The Maverick Law had been in effect for a few years. It was in July, right after spring roundup was over, and this group of six men decided they were goin' to accuse a woman of rustlin'."

"The one they called Cattle Kate."

"That was never her name, but that was the name they gave her after they hanged her and the man she was livin' with. Made her out to be a thief and a whore, and put it out in all the newspapers. You know, the cattlemen controlled a couple of the papers in Cheyenne, and then their version of the story got spread in newspapers all the way to Omaha and Chicago. Truth is, she had bought a bunch of sore-foot cattle from an emigrant and had 'em in her pasture, but she was havin' a hard time applyin' for her own brand. Another little instance of how the Association controlled things. Meanwhile, one of these six men wanted the land she was on, and he made her an offer, and she turned him down. So when roundup was over, he and his cohorts took it upon themselves to hang her and her husband, scare off some witnesses, and dispose of others. And lo and behold, the man who wanted her land ended up filing on it after all."

"I've never heard the whole story."

Macmillan waved his hand. "That's just the first part. Once the cattlemen saw that they could get away with it, they got bolder. Another bunch of 'em, including officers of the Association, put together the invasion. That happened. In '92."

"I've heard of the invasion, or the Johnson County War, as they call it."

"Everyone has. But not everyone sees it as a big crooked deal, which it was, sanctioned by the acting governor. Brazen as hell. They worked up a story about a big rustler problem, and they used that as a justification to bring in their army of gun hands. They wanted to exterminate some men and run off as many of the others as they could. They had a big plan and a long dead list. This is all on the record."

"Just to control the range?"

"To begin with. But when one of their attacks didn't work out, they had to get rid of witnesses who knew who was behind it. And just like the Cattle Kate incident, they ran this thing out, and no one went to court for it. Took longer, and they had more help, but they got it done."

"Whew."

"I get worked up talkin' about it, and I try not to. But the truth is, they keep gettin' away with it."

Del and Macmillan crossed the creek and split up, as they had been told to do. Before long, Del was trotting and loping his horse to catch up with cattle and read their brands. About a fourth of the cow-calf pairs he saw carried the Spoke brand—a hub with a club-like spindle and a small arc to represent part of the wagon rim. He did not see any pairs with mismatched brands.

The cattle were in their natural state and acted as always. They did not seem to have been spooked or harried. The cows lumbered at a trot, their bellies jiggling and their teats swaying. The calves ran and kicked up their hind legs. Cows drooled and mooed. Calves blatted and bawled. Rear ends large and small were spattered with shiny green manure. Flies hovered. For this, Del thought, men were willing to frame and kill one another.

★ ★ ★ ★ ★

Overlin sat at the bunkhouse table, biding his time as the hired men ate their fried bacon and potatoes. He stared at the cup of coffee in front of him as he rubbed the tuft of hair on the bare spot on top of his head.

Westfall was the first to finish, as usual. He put his plate and fork in the wreck pan and carried his coffee cup to his bunk. Seated, he took off his spectacles and wiped them with a white handkerchief.

Macmillan finished next, and as he stood up, the boss spoke.

"Mac, I'll have you ride out by yourself again. I've got a separate job for Del." Overlin picked up his coffee cup and held it close to his mouth. He did not look straight at either of them. "Del, we need to get a start on the chuck wagon. I know roundup's a ways off, but I don't want to put it off until the last minute in case something like an axle needs to be repaired. To begin with, you can spread out the canvas fly. Air it out, and fix any holes in it. I know it's got at least a couple."

"I'll need some repair stuff—needle and thread."

"Rucker can tell you where to find it." Overlin took a sip of coffee and spoke in a more relaxed tone to Price. "Jim, you and Ed can go south and east. Same as always. Keep an eye out."

"We'll do it."

Del thought of his spurs. He wouldn't need them, and they would get in the way when he laid out the big canvas sheet and crawled around to work on it.

As he sat on his bunk and unbuckled his spurs, he had the strange feeling that he and Macmillan were being separated because they had talked about the boss. He shook his head. It couldn't be. They had ridden out almost a mile before they said a word, and they hadn't talked about crooked cattlemen until they had reached Coldwater Creek. Now that he thought of it, it wasn't the first time the boss had split them up. Maybe the boss wanted to come around and quiz him again.

He found the needles and thread where Rucker told him they would be, in a cubbyhole inside the chuck wagon. He took the large folded bundle of canvas from the bed of the wagon and spread it on the barn floor. The smell of dust and smoke came out. The sheet was about twelve feet by fifteen and of medium weight. It made a useful canopy, and it worked better if it didn't have leaks, so at least he felt useful. Envisioning the work ahead, he decided he would use a wood chip in the heel of his hand to push the big needle through the double thicknesses of canvas.

He found a couple of chips at the woodpile. Returning to the barn, he set up a wooden box where the sunlight streamed through the doorway. Seated, he rolled out a six-foot length of thread from the spool, cut it, doubled it, and threaded the folded end through the large eye of the three-inch needle. He tied the loose ends into a knot and now had a four-ply length to stitch up the first hole.

A shadow on the floor caused him to turn. Lawna stood in the doorway, wearing a plain, pale green dress and bonnet. She rubbed her hands as if she was wiping away the crumbs of toast, and motioning with her head at the rumpled sheet of canvas, she said, "Are you working on your trousseau?"

It caught him off guard, and he laughed. Risking a joke, he said, "For bundling."

She raised her eyebrows, and her blue eyes had a shine. "I think there's an old saying about the more times you fold a blanket, but that's about cousins marrying." She took a short breath. "I saw you out looking for grasshoppers, and I wondered what you were doing."

"I was picking up a couple of wood chips to use as a thimble." He held up the needle with the thread dangling.

"I saw you threading it, but I waited to see how many tries it would take."

60

"How did I do?"

She pursed her lips and released them. "All right. By the time you get to the smaller work, like embroidering your dishcloths, you'll be working with smaller needles and finer thread. Can I give you a hand with anything?"

"It might help. A couple of the holes in the middle of the sheet might be clumsy for one person."

"I could throw a stitch in it for you, but you need the practice."

"We actually do a bit of sewing. Not just rough work like this, but mending shirts and such."

"I know. And sewing sacks in the grain harvest."

"Quite a few of the sack sewers are women, though men do it, too." An image of Clede passed through his mind. "Of course, the sack jigs, the ones who handle the sacks for filling and stacking, are men."

"Women have always worked in the fields," she said. "From the time of Ruth. There are probably some of them stomping grapes in France and Italy at the moment. Or picking up almonds in Spain. I saw a delightful photograph of a crew of Spanish girls sitting in the shade of an orchard with their baskets. Some of them were very pretty."

Del cast a glance at her pale green dress and bonnet, and he thought her clothing might have done for a peasant woman in an old painting, but he could not see her in that role. He picked up the edge of the canvas and began working his way toward a rip. Without looking at her, he said, "I was told that you picked a few chokecherries when you were younger."

She blew a breath upward. "I can imagine who told you. Well, I won't say anything about your boss."

"I think that if you hold the canvas right here, I can pull it out straight on the other side, and I can fold it so the rip goes from fold to fold. Then I can sew it up."

She moved close to him and took the canvas in her hands. He moved to the other side of the tear, and they folded the sheet. Del pushed the needle through the fold and then began stitching the torn edges together. The needle went through the canvas well enough that he did not think he would need a makeshift thimble.

Lawna said, "My father liked to work with his hands. He braided leather and that sort of thing. I have a quirt he made. Most of the other things are not around anymore."

"Oh."

She had a sulky tone as she said, "Someone got rid of them."

"Do you remember your father very well?"

"Not much at all. One memory that stays with me is when I went out to watch him clear snow from the doorstep and the walkway. He held a big shovelful of snow right up to my face and then tossed it aside."

Del continued stitching, moving his left hand toward her as he held the fringed fabric edges together. "It's good to remember what we can."

She did not move. "They were friends, you know."

"Who were?"

"He and Bill."

Her curt pronunciation of her stepfather's name gave him a second's pause. He pulled the needle through and tightened the stitch. "I didn't know that." He moved his thumb another half-inch to the left. "Let me take a couple of more wraps, and I'll tie it off."

He cut a new length of thread, doubled it, and threaded the needle for the next repair. The two of them took up the canvas as before and folded it. Del found a starting place and pushed the needle. The sharp, shiny point came through, and he pulled it. The thread followed. He could feel her soft breath, and he spoke to break the silence.

"Have you made jelly yet?"

"Oh, yes. We didn't get much, but it's in the jars."

He stitched along. "Do you put up anything else?"

"Sometimes my mother gets wild plums from the old place down south, and we make jam. Some years there's no plums, and some years she can't get anyone to bring her any."

"They make good jam, don't they?"

"Oh, yes. And pies."

She was not moving away. He thought she might even have inched closer. As he held the fold at the end of the stitch, he felt her upper body against his arm. She took a full breath, then held still as he took a couple of overlapping stitches at the end and tied a double knot with the needle.

"You're doing well," she said.

"I have good help."

The tinkle of a bell sounded.

"That's for me," she said. "Someone doesn't like me to be gone for very long."

"Thanks for your help."

"Don't mention it. Next time, we'll build a circus tent."

Overlin came to the bunkhouse to smoke his pipe after supper. Del was wondering about the wild plums in the place farther south when the boss blew out a cloud of smoke and said, "Boys, we've got a job that'll take us away for a couple of days. So you might think about what you want to take with you in the morning. Figure two nights. You'll camp out." He put his thumb over the bowl of the pipe and puffed. "Up north a ways, near the bend in the creek, but on this side. I want to fence off an area, a hundred feet by a hundred feet, where we can put in some haystacks."

Price said, "So we're gonna have to load up posts and wire

and diggin' bars and the whole shebang. Hammers and steeples. Shovels."

"That's right. You won't get started on it until tomorrow afternoon, and I figure it'll take about a day and a half. Some of the digging might be hard, and the tamping, too." Overlin looked around at the four men. "Not very complicated. I'll go up there with you to make sure you put it in the right spot, and then I'll trust you to get it done on your own."

Del did not ask, but he did not think that the site for the fence lay on deeded land. But it was not marking a boundary for possession, or controlling water, or excluding anyone from anything except for a small plot. In the middle of such a broad expanse of grassland, the area looked small indeed—not much larger than a house. The wind and the dust and the grasshoppers would go right through the walls of wire, once they were up. Right now, with only the corner posts in place, and the grass already showing wear from all the back-and-forth movement of measuring and squaring the corners, the place might be mistaken by Easterners for a large outdoor boxing ring.

Men who worked with cattle, however, observed a significant difference between fencing in and fencing out. All of the wire on this little structure would go on the outsides of the posts, to keep out cattle and other grazing animals, such as horses, mules, and sheep. Deer would jump over the wire, and antelope would crawl under. All of these considerations had been worked over, especially by Price and Macmillan, as the men walked back and forth and conferred during the layout. Now they were lining up and marking the spots for the posts in between the corners—six on each side, a little less than fifteen feet apart.

Del carried the posts from the wagon and laid them in place as Price and Macmillan did the measuring and sighting in. Westfall marked the spots with a shovel. The voices of the men and the stamping and snorting of the tied horses made a small impression in the wide-open setting. Del was used to scenes on the range being filled with mooing and lowing cattle, and he did not miss them now. Nor did he miss the dust and the flies. For the time being, he could enjoy the simplicity, even as the hot sun bore down.

Shadows were reaching out from the sagebrush as Price built up a small fire with wood they had brought from the ranch. Westfall drew out a knife that he carried in a sheath on his left hip, and with an intent gaze through his spectacles, he made serious work of slicing salt pork. By the time the sun had slipped behind the distant mountains, the pork was spluttering in the large black skillet. Price set out a stack of tin plates and a cotton sack full of cold biscuits.

"This ain't the Diamond Palace," he said, "but the grub smells good to me."

"Me, too," said Macmillan.

After flipping the pork a couple of times, Price lifted a slice with his knife and set it onto a tin plate. "I don't know what time the girls'll show up. I hope they don't get lost in the dark." He handed the plate to Westfall.

"That's always a danger," said Macmillan.

"The ones that wear bright colors seem to thrive in the bright lights."

"Some of them do good work in the dark."

Price handed the next plate to Del. "Not all of them?"

Macmillan took the tone of the man who knew something of the world. "Nah, not all of 'em. There's the ones that don't undress all the way. They leave their underclothes on one leg. And others, they just lay there and stare at the ceiling, like they're gettin' a tooth pulled out."

Price had a look of mild surprise as he handed the next plate to Macmillan, but he spoke as if he was a man of experience. "That's human nature. Not everyone's the same." He served himself and set the skillet off to the side of the fire. "There's a second slice for everyone. And plenty of biscuits. What about you, Del?"

"I'll have some more in a minute."

"I mean about the girls."

"Oh, I don't know very much. I'm still learning."

"Like Ed and me."

Westfall did not look up as he said, "Don't worry about me."

Price said, "That's all right. It's all in fun. I don't mean any harm."

Macmillan said, "None of us means any malice. I was just answering your question. Even if I speak lightly of some of them, those girls are all just trying to make a living. I don't begrudge any of 'em, at least the ones I know. Now the ones that work in crooked places, where they put knockout drops in your drink and all of that, I don't have anything to do with them."

"It's a good way to be. Stay out of trouble. That's the good part of life out on the range."

Del thought, *There's trouble enough there, too,* but he did not think he had to say it. He did not want to volunteer anything to the main topic anyway, and he was glad that Price did not bring him into it.

Work slowed down with the digging of the holes the next day. As the boss had anticipated, the ground was dry and hard. The crew had only one digging bar, so Del and Westfall took turns chipping out small pieces of tan, clayish material. When they had the post in the hole, they took turns tamping. One person had to hold the post because it shifted so much with the hard packing that was necessary. Price and Macmillan kept busy at building diagonal corner braces and a wire gate.

By midday, the men had all the posts up on two sides.

"The boss was right," said Price. "We'll be the rest of the day gettin' those other posts put in. We can string the wire one side at a time, but I don't think we'll be picking up everything until tomorrow morning."

As Price built a fire for the noon meal, Westfall went to work on a chunk of beef that had been wrapped in cloth and stored at the bottom of the supplies and bedrolls. He took out his sheath knife, rolled his sleeves up above his elbows, and concentrated on cutting the meat into cubes. Macmillan looked after the horses, and Del went to the creek for a bucket of water.

With the fire burned down, Price set the skillet on the stove. The grease from that morning's bacon melted, and the red cubes of meat went in. Westfall's pale, slender arms were turning pink, so he rolled down his sleeves. He peeled and diced three onions and scraped all the white pieces onto the top of the sizzling meat.

Price held a small saltbox in one hand and scattered pinches of salt with the other. "This is going to be good grub," he said.

With no scarcity of water, the men rinsed their faces in the basin and dried off in the sunlight. Del set out for the creek for more water.

The stream ran clearer here where it ran out of the canyon than it did downstream, where it picked up dirt and runoff along the way. Del dipped the bucket with its back to the current, as he had learned, to get less debris, and pulled up the dripping weight. As he walked up the bank, he felt a tightening in his stomach at the sight of two horsemen riding into the camp. He knew them in the instant that he saw them. Hardesty and Fisher.

The two visitors had dismounted and had tied their horses to a wagon wheel by the time Del walked into camp with the bucket of water. He exchanged a minimal greeting with each of them.

Price said, "Looks like you made it just in time for dinner. Did you whip the horses?"

"We didn't know you were here," said Hardesty.

"Just the two of you. We'll have enough to go around. Where's Hilton?"

The air went dead for a second until Fisher said, "He ain't here anymore."

"There's more water. Get cleaned up if you want. The basin's over there."

"Do you have enough plates?" asked Hardesty.

"We've got a whole stack. That way we don't have to clean 'em but once a day."

Del had an uneasy feeling in his midsection, a mixture of dislike and dread. Fisher had his brown hat cocked back on his head. He had a way of staring past Del, as if to ignore him, while his crooked lower lip, moist with tobacco juice, made him appear ready for an insolent comment. Every time Del saw Fisher, he remembered spring roundup and the man's series of lewd remarks about doing things with chickens. In addition, when Fisher was not on horseback, such as now, he had the habit of crossing his arms and flexing his muscles.

Del did not find Hardesty's company any more pleasant. The foreman of the Pyramid had a humorless, almost lethargic, air about him today, and as usual, he looked past Del as if he was not present. Hardesty was also wearing his large-roweled spurs, which clinked as he moved around in his swaggering way.

Price crouched to stir the meat and onions. The aroma of the cooking food rose on the air. "Just a little longer," he said as he stood up.

Del noticed that neither of the visitors bothered to wash up. That was fine with him. He would just as soon not have carried water for them.

Westfall and Macmillan stood near the back of the wagon where the tin plates were stacked on the tailgate. Silence weighed on the air until Price spoke again.

"You boys out checkin' on cattle, as usual?"

Hardesty said, "We do our work."

Price had a cheery tone as he said, "So do we. Had a peaceful time in camp last night." He smiled at Fisher in the way of one who shared knowledge or the same topic of humor. "We waited all night for the girls, but they never showed up."

Fisher said, "They never do. Little whores play hard to get."

"Not all of 'em. Some of 'em are as sweet as punkin pie."

"Or a peach with the pit taken out."

Hardesty scowled at Fisher, who pushed up his lower lip.

Price missed the exchange, as he squatted to stir the skillet again. He stood up, still smiling. "Yep. I was quizzin' the boys on it last night. Always got somethin' to learn, somethin' to look forward to."

Del thought, *Just quit. Please.*

"Like you said, sweet as a peach. Gives you somethin' to think about. Like I heard in a song. 'When you're comin' through the gol-den gate—' "

Hardesty exploded. He let out a large, seething breath as he landed a punch on Price's left jaw. Price stumbled backward and fell on his hip and elbow.

Del stared, but only for a second, because Hardesty turned and punched him as well. Del felt the fist slam into the side of his face, and his feet went out from under him. As he gathered his senses, he did not think he had given Hardesty any reason, so he imagined Hardesty was not satisfied with punching just one person. Furthermore, Hardesty was not standing over him but had stepped aside.

Macmillan helped Del up but made no move to intervene.

Price pushed himself up onto his feet alone.

Hardesty said, "That's all for today. Let's go, Al." His spurs jingled as he stomped away.

Fisher had a nonchalant air as he caught up. The two of them untied their horses and led them away a few paces. Hardesty grabbed his saddle horn and cantle and pulled himself aboard, while Fisher bounced off his right foot, stabbed the stirrup with his left, and made a flying mount. The men rode away in a gallop.

Price had his eyes wide open as he rubbed his jaw. "Boy, he sure got sore. You'd think maybe he's not gettin' what he wants, and he takes it out on everyone else."

"Huh," said Macmillan. "You've just got to watch what you say around some people. Like you said last night, stay out of trouble."

Westfall stepped forward and said, "To hell with them."

"That's right," said Price. "At least they didn't eat any of our grub. We've got plenty to go around, like we planned to begin with."

CHAPTER FIVE

Del stood outside in back of the bunkhouse and watched the sun clear the hills to the east. The morning air was fresh and clean, and the dry grass of late summer was soft under his feet. The rain had not been as heavy as the week before, but it had drizzled late enough to keep the boys from going to town. With the clear blue sky above, Sunday was looking better. Del confirmed a thought he had considered the night before when the light rain was pattering on the roof—he could ride his own horse today.

The sun had risen in the sky by the time he had breakfast behind him and was headed for the horse pasture, halter in hand. Conscious of not tearing his shirt, he opened and closed the pasture gate rather than climb through the barbed-wire strands. As he walked across the cropped grass and scanned the grazing animals, one horse after another raised its head.

A sorrel with a blaze faced him, and its white socks in front came into view as the horse detached itself from the others. Del smiled and called, "Come here, Brush."

The horse and its owner walked toward one another in the open pasture. Del noted the narrow blaze—a white strip in the shape of an artist's paintbrush—and the matching white socks. Having his own horse was one of the gifts of life. Some men took it for granted, but Del reminded himself time and again that there were many people in cities and small towns and little dirt farms who wished they could have a horse, like he had with Brush.

He put his arms around Brush's neck, passed the lead rope from his left hand to his right, draped the rope over the mane, and slipped the halter onto the horse's muzzle. With the gentle sun shining on them both, they headed for the barn and the hitching rail.

Using a steel currycomb with teeth rising from the back side, Del combed and brushed his horse. Next came the blanket and pad, followed by the saddle. He drew the latigo and tightened the front cinch, then buckled the rear cinch. After loosening the halter, he draped the bridle into place and slipped the bit over the lower teeth until a wrinkle formed at the corner of Brush's mouth. Del pulled the ears through the headstall and patted the shiny neck.

"Good boy," he said.

He tucked the halter into the saddlebag and led the horse out a few steps. He set his reins in place, put his foot in the stirrup, grabbed the saddle horn, and swung aboard. Brush stood still until Del caught his right stirrup, and they were ready to go.

The clip-clop of hooves was softer than usual, thanks to the overnight rain. Del wondered if Lawna heard or saw him riding out of the yard. He did not think he had any real prospects with her. His interpretation was that she was flirting with him as a safeguard, to keep herself from committing all the way to Rich Hardesty. The Pyramid foreman, in turn, might well be receiving small rebuffs. Del did not think the punch in the jaw was anything personal. Price had made the ill-advised remark, and Del was just the next one at hand. He was convinced that if Lawna had a real interest in him, he would know it, and a single punch wouldn't drive him away. As it was, he thought it was a good use of his time, and of a fresh shirt, to ride a ways north where a dark-haired girl wore a red ribbon in her hair.

As he had not started early and did not push his horse, the sun had climbed to late morning when he stopped at Coldwater Creek. His route took him east of the site where they built the haystack enclosure, and it would take him east of the spot where Holt Warren had met his end. If there was anything good in seeing Hardesty and Fisher a few days back, it was in learning that Hilton had left. On second thought, Del recalled that the information had come from Fisher, so he wondered how reliable it was.

Del and Brush did not cast much of a shadow as they came to a stop in the Wiggins farmyard. The heat of day was building, and the whitewashed buildings gleamed. The front door opened in the shade of the porch, and Wiggins stepped out in a halting, side-by-side step. He raised his hand to his eyebrows to cut the glare.

"You came by yourself."

"Thought I would take my horse for a ride. During the week, I ride company horses, and I don't want him to get soft."

"Well, come on in. You're just in time. I've cooked a pot of stew."

"Thanks." Del dismounted and tied up, then followed Wiggins into the house.

Once inside, he blinked his eyes and flared his nostrils. A heavy smell of mutton hung on the air. Del looked around for Tess, but all he saw was Clede sitting at the table. The man was wearing a clean white shirt and brown suspenders, and he was clean-shaven.

"Sit down," said Wiggins. "We'll put another bowl on the table. Tess gets so busy with all of the work that I do some of the cookin'. Give her a Sunday off."

"That's good." Del took off his hat.

"I made a big pot. Meat wants to spoil in this hot weather if you don't use it soon enough."

"That's for sure."

"Been hot where you are?"

"Most of the time. We got a little relief last night with some rain. Did you have any up here?"

"Just a sprinkle."

Del exchanged a greeting with Clede as he took a seat.

Wiggins called out, "We're ready to eat!"

Del restrained himself from watching the doorway. A minute passed, and Tess appeared in a tan dress, carrying two steaming, cream-colored crockery bowls. She set one in front of her uncle and one in front of Clede.

"Good afternoon," she said, with barely a glance. "I'll have yours in a minute."

The smell of the stew wafted his way, and it rose stronger when Tess set a bowl in front of him. He looked up and smiled, and he thought he saw an apologetic expression on her face.

"Thank you," he said.

"You're welcome." She retreated to the kitchen.

She returned with a spoon, and he met her eyes in a quick exchange as he thanked her again.

Del braced himself and dug in for the first spoonful. He blew the steam away and took in a chunk of meat and a piece of onion. He almost gagged. The meat had a rancid taste that corresponded with the odor. He stole a glance at the other two at the table. Wiggins was eating with his mouth open, while Clede had his mouth pressed closed and was chewing with solemn motions.

"What news from down your way?" Wiggins asked.

Del did not talk much during bunkhouse and chuck wagon meals, but he realized he sat at a farmer's table, so in addition to eating what his host ate, he went along with the conversation. "Not much except the rain. We had a better shower about a week ago, but a few days later, we had to dig some postholes a few miles away, and the ground was as hard and dry as can be."

"That's the way it is. They say the rain falls on the just and the unjust alike, but you can get a good shower in one place, and it'll be dry as a bone a mile away. Same with hail."

"At least we didn't get hailed on, working out in the open."

Wiggins did not look up from eating. "Building fence?"

"Just a little square one, for haystacks."

"I didn't think cattlemen liked fences."

Clede spoke up. "They don't like anything."

"Sure they do," said Wiggins, with a little laugh. "They like money, just like we all do. If a fence'll help them make money, they'll put one in. Same as us."

Clede's eyelids remained half-closed. "There's a difference. They can pay someone else to do it."

"Well, you know damn well that some of us have to pay to get work done, else you wouldn't have any work for wages."

"It's not the same."

Wiggins's jowls sagged as he paused with his spoon upraised. "Maybe not. But I don't know any of us, especially those that've been here a while and stuck with it, that wouldn't like to be doin' a little better."

Clede tipped his head from one side to the other but did not answer.

Del made his slow way through the bowl of stew. The others finished theirs, and he felt obliged to do the same. He wondered why Tess did not join them, and he guessed that under the guise of letting men talk of their affairs, she was having bread and butter in the kitchen. When at last his bowl had nothing but glistening grease, he pushed it from him and breathed a sigh of relief. His stomach was churning, and he was afraid the mash would rise in his throat.

Tess appeared in the doorway, looking unharmed. "More?" she asked.

Clede shook his head.

"No, thanks," said Del.

Wiggins wiped his mouth with his hand. "I think you can take these bowls away."

"There's cake, you know."

"That can wait until later."

"Very well," she said. "I can wash the dishes in the meanwhile."

Clede scraped his chair backward as he stood up. "I'll help." He leaned over, gathered up the three bowls and spoons, and carried them to the kitchen.

Wiggins watched the doorway for a few seconds with a curious study. He reached into the pocket of his overalls, brought out a flask, and tipped himself a drink. He let out a long, sighing "Ahhh" as he screwed on the cap. "Kills the germs," he said.

Del nodded. He wondered how well whiskey would mix with the mess in his stomach, and he did not mind being left out.

"So," said Wiggins, "have you heard any more about this Holt Warren business?"

"There's been no talk about it at the ranch. A fellow in town told me that Warren knew Overlin and some of the others, at about the time Overlin got married the first time."

"Oh, yes. That wasn't too long after I first came here. I was younger then, so I got around more than I do now. Everyone knew the young couples, and they all knew each other, of course. With this bunch, at first it was Imogene, Diana, Holt, and Paul. They were all friends, and Bill came into their circle. If Holt had ever been more than friends with Imogene, Bill might not ever have worked his way in. But it was lopsided. Holt and Paul were both stuck on Diana. Little by little, things sifted down. The two young couples got married, and Holt got left out. He drew into himself and grubbed along, while the other two men each built up a ranch. Of course, that changed, too."

"You'd never know that Holt and Bill were friends at one time, from the little I saw."

"Hah. I don't know if they ever were. But then again, I didn't know any of 'em very well. I just knew who they were. But enough about them. What else is new?"

"Nothing that I can think of. Just work. None of us has been into town for more than a week now. The rain kept us home last night."

Wiggins wiped his mouth with his hand. "Just as well. That was one thing I learned. There was never as much in town as I hoped there would be. But there was devil enough. I saw many a man get separated from his money. Like they say, a fool and his money are soon parted. I don't know if that's in *Poor Richard's Almanack*, but he's got a lot of good advice in there, too. You're lookin' kind of green. Are you all right?"

Del had a dizziness in the head, and he was sure his stomach was going to revolt. He did not want such a thing to happen anywhere near here. He did not want Tess to remember that kind of an incident about him. "To tell you the truth, I do feel kinda woozy. I think I ought to be on my way before I'm any trouble to anyone."

"Maybe you should stay around and we can give you something. Castor oil, maybe."

Del pointed at his stomach. "I think I'd better leave before something happens."

Wiggins's face widened. "I understand. Sometimes even the most important of men have to be alone."

Del did not care to clarify which ailment he was dreading. He rose from his chair, and with his hat in his hand, he said,

John D. Nesbitt

"Please give my regards to Tess."

"I'll do that." Wiggins's eyes followed him.

Del made his way outside, where the hot sun almost knocked him down. He wasted no time in gathering the reins, leading the horse out, and climbing aboard. He fought down the internal eruption as he rode away.

Half a mile out, with the first rise of land behind him, he swung down and let it go. His stomach convulsed, and an ugly rush heaved out. His eyes watered. Sweat dripped from his face. He heaved a couple of more times and spit out as much of the taste as he could. He wiped his mouth and spit again.

He tipped his head back to take a reading of the sun. Not much past noon. Early yet. His thoughts traveled ahead, along the road to Provenance. As Wiggins said, there might be devil enough in town, but Del could imagine a couple of things that would settle the turmoil in his stomach.

Del did not bother to ask how cold the beer was. He ordered a glass and drank from it with appreciation. When Mitchell came around again, Del asked if there was anything to eat.

"I can't be fixing food," said the bartender. "I've got my hands full, and I'm in here alone on Sundays. I can order you a sandwich from the café, or you can go there yourself and have a bowl of stew."

"I'd like a sandwich to go with what I have here."

"Might take a few minutes. I'll send someone." Mitchell walked to the end of the bar and spoke across it to a man who sat by himself at a table with no overhead light. He was playing solitaire.

When the man stood up, Del saw that he was short and thick and about thirty-five years old. He put on a floppy, striped cap and headed for the door.

The stout man returned in a couple of minutes and resumed

78

his card game. He reached up as if to scratch his head, pulled off the cap, and scratched through his thick, dark hair.

About five minutes later, the front door opened with a rush of daylight. A boy about ten years old, wearing a white shirt and apron and a grain-colored newsboy cap, walked in with a dark, round tray in his hands.

Mitchell called out, "Over here, Jimmy," and pointed to Del.

The boy held up the tray, and Del took the object, which was wrapped in brown paper. The boy said, "Twenty-five cents."

Del had a two-bit piece ready. "Thanks," he said as he laid the coin on the tray.

"Tip him," said the bartender.

Del reached into his pocket and came out with a dime, which he set on the tray next to the quarter.

"Thanks, mister." The boy turned and walked away, carrying the coins on the tray.

Mitchell said, "You might buy Gil a glass of beer while you're at it." He motioned with his thumb toward the thickset man playing solitaire.

"Oh, sure." Del reached in and found another dime.

The sandwich was a plain combination of coarse brown bread and cold beef, but it went down all right with the help of the beer. Del ordered another glass. His stomach was feeling better, and his head was not as clouded as before.

He became aware of a small gathering of men at the far end of the bar. He had seen them when he came in, and he had had a sense of who they were, but in his dazed and miserable state, he had avoided looking at them. Now as their voices raised in good cheer, he recognized Norris Drayton, his pal Josh Crittenden, and the man who referred to them as the old liars' club, Malcolm Bain.

The man who had been playing solitaire stood up, put on his cap, and leaned forward to walk toward the door. After a few steps, he detoured to speak to Del. He had a short face, with heavy eyebrows, dark eyes, coarse stubble, and a small chin, which, along with his stocky build, reminded Del of a pug dog. He spoke in a courteous tone as he said, "Thanks for the glass of beer, mister."

"My thanks to you."

The man pulled the cap off his head and held out a thick hand to shake. "Gil Simms."

"Pleased to meet you. My name is Del Rowland. I work on a ranch hereabouts."

"So do I. That is, I work for a farmer." He put the cap back on his head. "Well, I'm on my way. Good to meet you."

"And the same to you."

The group at the end of the bar was going strong, with laughter and loud voices. A couple of minutes after Simms left, the voice of Norris Drayton carried down the bar. "Hey, cowboy, come down and have a drink with us."

As he was the only other patron in the saloon, Del could not ignore them, and he did not want to seem unfriendly. Also, it was early, and he did not think they would be very far into their cups. He finished his beer, pushed the glass away, and walked down the bar to join the merrymakers.

As soon as he reached the group, he saw that he was wrong, at least in the case of Malcolm Bain. The man with the cane had a relaxed expression on his face, with droopy eyes and a half-open mouth. He was wearing his cap and cloak, but he slumped on his dark cane and did not have the jaunty air of the man who had compared himself to a constable. Seeing Del, he raised his eyelids a fraction and said, "Stuck any pigs lately?"

"Don't mind him," said Drayton. "He's been up all night and hasn't been to bed yet."

"I see." Del turned to Josh Crittenden, who was dressed in a nondescript grey suit and a pale shirt with no tie. "How do you do? We met in here a while back."

"I'm doin' all right." He adjusted his glasses. "Can't complain. Doesn't do any good." He took a tight sip of whiskey. "You're young, but you'll find out for yourself."

Del was accustomed to older men who had a compulsion to share their wisdom with the young. He nodded and ordered a beer for himself.

Crittenden spoke again. "I mean it. It does no good to complain. When you're down, they kick you."

Drayton said, "This is the young fellow who was asking about Holt Warren."

Del flinched and was glad there was no one else in the saloon.

"I know," said Crittenden.

Malcolm Bain widened his eyes as if he was coming back into the conversation.

Crittenden said, "Holt Warren's a good example. Most men's problems come from women. If he hadn't been so stuck on a woman all that time, he wouldn't have been so glum, and for all we know, he wouldn't have put up such resistance when they came after him." He took another sip. "Every generation makes the same mistakes. Now you've got the foreman of another ranch running after the daughter and trying to prove himself with the man in charge. You find a man in trouble, or a man causin' trouble, and nine times out of ten you'll find a woman in the background."

Del had a picture of Lee Hilton, and he did not see a woman in it.

"Like I say, you're young, and like as not, you think I'm full of beans. Most of the time, people have to learn on their own, the hard way. Especially about women."

"Heh, heh," said Drayton. "Our young friend here is learning right along. Why, he met a charming woman in here just the other night."

"One way to learn," said Crittenden. "But don't think that payin' for it is the solution, either. A good many men have been killed in whorehouses, and in the alleys out back, and a good many more have gotten their dose of the clap and worse."

Light flowed into the saloon as the front door opened. A man in common working clothes and a slouch hat took his place at the end of the bar closest to the door.

"Who's that?" Del asked.

"Just someone who hangs around," said Drayton.

With a lull in the conversation, Crittenden started in again. "Sometimes you can't win. I've gone broke twice. Once I had a meat market with a partner, and his wife convinced him to run off with all the money. The second time, I had a harness shop. The fellow who worked for me got married, and the woman talked him into going into business for himself. I'll never know how much the woman did, but they stole all my customers, and then, when I was flat broke, they came back and bought me out for ten cents on the dollar." Crittenden sipped from his whiskey glass. "Now I work in a mercantile store. Thank God the man's wife stays in her place."

"Well," said Drayton, speaking to Del, "there you have another idea to consider about Holt Warren."

"I suppose so. Not much new, from what you told me before, and what I heard in another place. I understand that Holt Warren was friends with Paul Gresham in the early days."

"That's true. They were friends. A group of them. Bill Overlin made his way into the group. That was all pretty well known at the time."

Malcolm Bain spoke in a loud voice that made Del cringe. "You wanna talk about Bill Overlin and Holt Warren? Well, I'll tell you something. I know what that double-dealing son of a bitch did to Paul Gresham's Appaloosa horses."

"Shh-shh," said the old dentist. "Draw down a little. The

whole town can hear you."

"Let 'em. See if I care. This is a bacon gravy town. A horse tramples a bed of pansies, and they cry out loud. But the ruling class shoots down a peasant, they look the other way." The man's eyes were glassy, but they were wide open. "I'll tell you, I grew up in Pittsburgh, in a part of town that was all Paddies and Welshmen, and you had to be tough. Later on, I worked for a shoemaker in Milwaukee, about the time all the Bohunks came in, and the Polacks, and the next thing you knew, we were having labor riots just like in Chicago. And strike busters. You damn right it was tough, all the way around." He reached into his pocket and brought out a folding knife, which he opened with a flick of the wrist. He leveled his unsteady gaze at Del. "You know what I mean?"

Del shrugged. "I suppose."

"Some people have money, and some don't. I've always been broke. I've never had a fair chance. When all the other kids were running and jumping, I was leaning on my crutches. When they were riding horses, or later on, dancing, I was limping along and leaning on this cane. Oh, I can ride a horse, and I'll tell you it's easier than going on foot, but you won't see me in a parade."

"This is all fine," said Crittenden, "but what are you gettin' at?"

Bain glared at the older man. "What I'm saying is, not everyone gets an even chance. Not from the beginning, and not as you go along."

Crittenden made a backward wave with his hand. "Like I said, when you're down, they kick you."

Del pondered these men who seem compelled to tell their life stories and insist on their life philosophies. He wondered if it was a matter of getting drunk on a Sunday afternoon with the rest of the world outside or if they had said it all many times and were bringing it out for a new audience.

Norris Drayton took a tan cigarette from his case and lit it. "At least we're all still alive. It's more than I can say for our late friend."

His voice still loud, Malcolm Bain said, "Holt Warren was a friend of mine. A good friend. And I'm sick of all these mealy-mouths." He raised his fist to chin level. "I wish every one of those ruling-class pigs was strung up on a telegraph pole!"

Drayton blew away a quick puff of smoke. "Be careful with what you say."

"I'll say what I want." Bain reached for his glass of whiskey on the bar and tossed down the rest of the drink. He teetered as he set the empty glass on the bar top.

"You'd better sit down," said Drayton. "You're starting to wobble."

"I'm just fine."

"I know you, and I can tell. Sit down."

Crittenden and Drayton together helped the drunk man into the chair where Simms had sat earlier.

"He'll be all right," said Drayton. "He doesn't go to work again until tomorrow night."

Del finished his glass of beer. "Well, I have to work tomorrow morning, so this had better be it for me."

Drayton smiled. "It's better not to try to do it all at once."

Del observed Malcolm Bain. The drunk man's eyes were closed, his chin rested on his chest, and his head lolled. Del winced.

He took leave of the two men standing, nodded to the stranger at the other end of the bar, and walked out into the sunlight. He blinked his eyes, found his horse, and made ready to start for the ranch. *Bless the dogs and horses. They're always the same. Never change.*

CHAPTER SIX

Del was combing the mane on the grey horse when Lawna appeared in the morning sunlight dressed in a riding outfit. She stood on his side of the horse, by the hip.

"You're going with me today," she said.

He glanced over his shoulder. She was wearing a matching skirt and jacket of light brown with gold embroidery, a cream-colored blouse, and a straw hat with a small cluster of dried blue flowers in the hatband. The skirt was the kind that he had heard referred to as a shotgun riding skirt, as it had double-barreled leggings that reached to her boots. He met her blue eyes and said, "I haven't gotten my orders yet."

She smiled. "We were arguing about it. That's why he didn't go to the bunkhouse earlier."

"Here he comes. I'll wait to hear it from him."

Bill Overlin approached with a businesslike stride and stopped on the other side of the horse. "It looks like Missy got here first, but just to be clear, she and her mother think it might be time for the plums to be ripening." Overlin paused.

"It's the second of September," Del said.

"I know. What I was going to say is that the plums are down south, at the other place. You know the way there. She can show you where the plums are. They grow in a little drainage, actually a place where two draws come together. You'll see when you get there."

"Very good."

"Saddle the horse that she usually rides. The yellow one. She'll bring whatever you need—some canvas buckets and a lunch. But you don't need to be gone all day."

"Yes, sir."

Overlin walked away. Lawna beamed with a triumphant expression and seemed to grow an inch taller as she took in a breath. "I'll get the things," she said.

Del tipped his hat to keep the sun out of his left eye as he and Lawna rode south. The palomino wanted to step out, so Lawna kept fussing with the reins and scolding him. After about a mile, she spoke to Del.

"He didn't like it at all."

"Who?"

"Bill." The single syllable was like a stone that fell to the earth.

Del shrugged. "That's up to you folks."

"He said I went behind his back. But all I did was ask Jim and Ed, and they said they thought they had seen the plums and they thought they were getting ripe, and some had fallen to the ground. The plums don't ripen at exactly the same time every year, but it's usually around the first days of September."

Del glanced at her reins to see if she was keeping them even.

"He doesn't like it because it was my father's place. You know, he had all the buildings torn down and the lumber hauled away. And yet my mother and I have always lived in the house where Imogene lived."

Del kept his eyes on the trail ahead. "I don't know much about that."

"I don't know everything."

Del was not sure of what to make of her comment. He could tell she still had her dander up, and he thought it would be better not to stoke the fire. "Are your stirrups adjusted all right?" he asked.

"Oh, yes. I never change them, and no one else uses this saddle. My mother quit riding a long time ago."

"I couldn't tell how much you had your knees bent. Maybe it's the ruffles on your legs."

"Don't get started on that."

"I didn't mean to."

"Rich says they make me look like Mother Featherlegs. He doesn't know. He never saw her. He just repeats what he's heard."

Del had heard the stories as well about the madam who ran a roadhouse near Silver Springs on the old Cheyenne-to-Deadwood stage route. "I wouldn't say anything like that."

"You'd better not. There's enough uncouth people around here as it is."

"I just wanted to make sure you were riding all right. It's about five miles down there and five miles back, so it would be a good time to tune things up with your horse. Make sure your seat is good, keep your reins even, make sure he does everything you say."

"I do. But he's not a piano."

"I know. But sometimes you make 'em do things just to have them do what you tell 'em. So if you want to trot out ahead, or put him in a circle, or anything like that, go ahead."

"I will."

They found the plums as Lawna had expected—ripening and beginning to fall. The fruit was not large, about the size of the last joint of a lady's thumb—and the ripe ones were shaded yellow and light purple. Lawna had brought four canvas buckets with rope handles and canvas-wrapped rope rims. She held each bucket while Del worked with both hands, holding a branch and picking the plums. The ripe ones fell off with a slight nudge, so she stood close and held the bucket beneath his hands. In some places, he picked with both hands. At times he had the leaves between him and her, and at times he was close enough to feel her breath. The ripe plums had a sweet aroma, which rose up from the canvas cylinder as the fruit accumulated.

They filled the four buckets in about an hour. A canvas bucket of water had to be hung from a tree, but these sat on the ground like small bags of potatoes. Del set the four of them together in the shade as Lawna spread a canvas sheet on the ground and set out their lunch.

As Del took a seat, he said, "This work goes a lot faster than the chokecherries, especially with two people."

"It's hardly work," she said. "But it's not like the berry-picking parties I've heard of, by cool mountain streams."

"It all has its charm."

"Yes, in a way. Though it's bittersweet for me. Like I said before, this was my father's place. This is where he and my mother came when they first married and where they . . . had me." She handed Del a sandwich wrapped in a white cloth. "Sometimes I think about taking this place back, but I don't know how I would do it. And they seem to have other plans for me."

"They?"

"Bill, and to some extent, my mother. She goes along. She says I can't expect to do much better." Lawna unwrapped a sandwich for herself.

"You said something to that effect the other day."

"Well, he set it up, and she has a hard time going against him on anything. I think the more time a person is in a situation like that, the harder it is to change it."

"Could be."

"But that's them. I don't want to fall into the same thing, but right now, I don't see any easy way out. You think of things, like a boulder falling from the sky."

"That doesn't happen very often."

"Hardly at all."

They ate their sandwiches, and Del wondered what else she had in the cloth bag.

"You're wondering what's in there." She smiled, and her eyes sparkled. "I won't keep you in suspense. I brought two cans of peaches, one for each of us. They're the smaller size. That way, I won't contaminate you, and you won't contaminate me."

"I'll be happy to open both of them. Do we bend the lids and use them for spoons?"

"This is not the Brown Palace Hotel, but I did bring spoons."

Del laughed.

"It's a first-class hotel in Denver."

"Oh, I know that. It just reminded me of something Jim Price said when he was frying pork in a skillet. He said, 'This ain't the Diamond Palace.'"

She laughed. "Well, it's not that, either. If you want to drink the juice from the can, I will look the other way."

"I'll do the same."

When they were finished with the meal and Lawna had things put away, she sat back with both hands holding her up. Her straw hat sat on the ground next to her, and her clean blond hair hung past her shoulders. Her chest rose as she took a breath. She said, "It's so peaceful here. I haven't heard another sound all the time we've been here."

"It's very nice."

"And he didn't want us to come down here. He's just jealous, afraid of anything from the past. You know, he was supposedly a friend of my father."

"I think I heard something like that."

Her blue eyes had a look of exasperation. "I don't know if he ever had a friend. Bill, that is. He had no scruples about taking everything my father left. He tore everything down, and on top of that, he sold my father's prized horses."

"Really?"

"Yes. They were Appaloosas. My mother had to grit her teeth."

"Oh."

"I don't think he cared. I don't think he cares about anybody but himself. He's hollow and rotten. Sometimes I think he has no soul." She shook her head, and her hair waved. She sat straight up and looked at Del. "I know you won't repeat any of this, ever."

He shook his head. "Of course not. Never a word."

"I just wish I could take this place back. I don't know if I stand a better chance of doing it by marrying what's-his-name or by holding out."

"I couldn't tell you. I don't know anything."

"Everyone knows something."

"Well, yes." He opened and closed his hand.

"What's the matter?"

"This might be an odd time to say it, but I'd like to rinse my hands. They got sticky with those plums, and a bit of juice dripped from the lid of the can." He motioned with his hand toward his canteen, which sat on the canvas between them. "I've got plenty of water left. If you could splash a few drops, it would help."

She rolled over onto her knees, picked up the canteen, and walked on her knees to the edge of the canvas. "Over here?"

"Fine," he said. He rose, walked, and kneeled. He held his hands out, and she poured a trickle.

Her face was not a foot away from his when she turned and said, "More?"

"That's enough, I think."

"Would you do the same for me?"

"Sure." He took the canteen and poured water onto her well-kept hands.

She smiled and said, "Do you let a girl drink from your canteen?"

"Of course." He handed it to her.

She took a sip, replaced the cap, and set the canteen aside. She was facing him with one arm open. With her other hand, she took his.

Del found the liberty to think for himself as he unsaddled, brushed, and put away the grey and the palomino. All the way back to the ranch, he and Lawna had spoken very little, and when they did, it was about which way to go or how to keep the plums from spilling. Now, with Lawna and the four canvas buckets safe in the kitchen, his thoughts ran free.

He tried to grasp the largeness of what he had done. It had not taken long, even with the bit of tenderness afterwards—not enough to affect anyone's calculation of how long they were gone. In a way, it was a hidden moment, a secret treasure that two people shared in a secluded scene of nature.

On the other hand, it was something big and something he could not undo. He recalled a similar feeling when he shot a big deer and watched it fall to the ground, its antlers sticking up above the sagebrush. He imagined it was akin to the feeling a person had after killing another human. Maybe it would remain a secret, and maybe it would get out.

If Overlin found out, which Del did not think likely, at least for a while, he would fire Del in an instant. That would not be so bad, as Del assumed it was a matter of time until he left anyway. As he answered the question to himself, the main reason he had stayed had been to learn more of the story behind Holt Warren—that, and as he admitted to himself, the prospect of something with Lawna.

He did not think that he and Lawna had moved closer to any real romance. To the contrary, he had a sense that she had entered into their moment of intimacy with a set of motives that might not have been very conscious. Some of it may have been pure physical attraction and impulse, but she was not a trollop or a slattern. She was selective, although he did not think she was calculating. He believed she was spiting her stepfather, for it was clear that she despised him. She might also be fortifying herself against Hardesty, as if by giving some of herself to Del, she could keep from committing herself to the man picked out for her. As to whether Hardesty had been shut out, always or just in the recent past, as suggested by Price's comment, Del preferred not to speculate. He was quite sure, however, that he was not Lawna's first experience of that nature.

He came back to wondering how much Lawna cared for him. He couldn't help it. Even if he knew she had used him in a way, he wanted to see her again. At the same time, he knew it was like riding a big horse that could blow up and break loose at any time. Everything he was hoping to accomplish, including the gathering of more knowledge about the Holt Warren affair, would be blown to hell.

Rucker was serving oatmeal mush with raisins when Overlin made his morning appearance. The boss did not take off his peaked hat as he stood close to the table.

Rucker said, "You're here early. Did you come to eat?"

Overlin shook his head. "No, thanks. I've got a lot to do, and I wanted to get this part out of the way." He paused for a second. "Jim and Ed, go south again. Same as always. Del and Mac, I want you to go to the Pyramid. They've got some horses with my brand that the men brought in, and I need to have them brought over here."

Macmillan turned in his seat. "What horses would they be?"

Overlin waved his hand. "I don't know. Some of mine. I would guess they've been out all winter and didn't get brought in during the spring."

"How many are there?"

"Three. What does it matter?"

Macmillan shrugged. "I was just wondering how many we could have missed when we brought 'em in."

"The numbers are never the same. We hardly ever bring in as many as we turned out in the fall. That's what it costs me not to keep 'em in and feed 'em all winter. Some die, some get stolen, and some hide out."

"We'll bring 'em in."

"I hope so. That's why I'm sending you over there." The boss shifted his weight, turned, and walked out.

Price raised his eyebrows as he passed the canned milk. "Looks like someone's not in a good mood today."

Rucker whacked the metal spoon on the lip of the pot. "He'll get over it. He's just got a lot on his mind. It's part of runnin' an outfit."

Del and Macmillan rode into the Pyramid ranch yard in the middle of the morning. The ground was dry and hard, and the horse hooves made a sharp clacking sound. Al Fisher stepped out of the bunkhouse, wearing his brown hat with a rounded crown. He set it back on his head, folded his arms, and said, "What do you need?"

Macmillan answered. "Boss sent us over to fetch some horses you picked up."

Fisher spat tobacco juice off to the side. "Don't know who said we picked 'em up, but there's three in the krell that's got his brand on the hip." He looked up with the vacant stare that he practiced.

The door of the bunkhouse opened, and spurs jingled. Rich Hardesty came out at a brisk pace, putting on his dull black hat. He squinted in the bright daylight as he spoke to Macmillan. "You come for the horses?"

"Yes, we did."

"They're over there. You can tell easy enough that they've been out. They haven't been combed or rode for a long while. Got chipped feet."

"Thanks. We brought ropes."

"They're all yours." Hardesty pivoted and walked back into the bunkhouse.

Del wondered if Hardesty avoided looking at him because of the incident at the fence-building camp, but he concluded that the foreman was treating them both as if they were insignificant.

Del and Macmillan turned their horses and headed toward the hitching rail in front of the barn. Fisher followed on foot. As they tied their horses, Fisher's voice came up behind them.

"Wanna see what I got?"

Macmillan looked over his shoulder. "What's that?"

"In here." Fisher kept walking toward the barn.

Del and Macmillan followed as Fisher opened the door and let the light in. They stopped when he did.

A four-point mule deer buck, greyish-brown and gruesome, hung by the neck from a yellow hemp rope. It had been field-dressed, and dried blood showed where it had been cut open.

Fisher crossed his arms and leaned back. "Got him this morning. One shot."

"Good for you," said Macmillan.

"Dick says it's a waste of time."

"Not everyone cares for hunting."

"Just as well," said Fisher. "You don't have everyone else out there tryin' to kill the big ones."

With his eyes adjusted, Del let his gaze travel around the

interior of the barn. Everything looked normal, with saddles and bridles and halters hanging on racks and pegs. He stopped and came back to a saddle with tapaderos. He thought it was the same one he had seen Hilton using, but that was no clear evidence that the man was still around. For all he knew, Hilton didn't even have his own saddle. Still, it was a detail to remember.

As the three of them walked toward the door, Del said to Fisher, "Keeping busy?"

"Oh, yeah." Fisher pushed his cheek out with his tongue. "Work never stops. If it ain't one thing, it's another."

Del imagined Hardesty drinking coffee in the bunkhouse, perhaps with other company.

Fisher continued. "Barely got time to pull the weed."

Del wished he had not said a thing.

"We'll get those horses," said Macmillan.

"Sure. I'll stand by in case you need a hand."

Del and Macmillan roped the three horses in short order, put halters and lead ropes on them, and set out for home. When they were well out of range, Del said, "What did you think of Hardesty?"

"Too busy for us. They work so hard, you know. If it ain't one thing, it's two."

"That's what it seemed like to me. And Fisher has time to hunt."

Macmillan said, "I don't like to hang a deer that way, but I shouldn't be so quick to criticize."

"Neither do I, but that's up to him."

Del and Macmillan took turns leading the third horse. The job went much slower than herding a bunch of horses, which entailed riding fast. Herding was questionable with these three, as they had been on the loose for a while and might like to return to their fugitive life. So the progress was slow, and the sun was hanging straight up when the group reached Coldwater Creek.

The men let the horses drink, and after some resistance, they got all the animals across the creek. Macmillan was leading two, and Del was leading one.

Less than a mile later, as they rode southeast, Del glanced over his left shoulder and saw a dark column of smoke in the north. "Look over there," he said as he reined to a stop.

The two led horses bunched up on Macmillan as he stopped. "Looks like it's in one place, not spread out like a grassfire."

Del said, "I think one of us should go take a look at it." He did not know whose property, if any, the fire was on, or whether it was moving onto grass, but fighting a fire was everybody's job.

Macmillan held out his hand. "Give me your rope if you want to, and I'll hold all three."

Del handed him the lead rope and took off. The bay he was riding stretched out its legs and covered the ground. As Del took his bearings, he thought he might be heading toward Holt Warren's place. The smoke was still going straight up, and the fire line was not moving.

After going uphill and down a couple of times, he came to a broad area and saw the fire ahead of him. He had guessed right. The house and stable he had seen on the earlier visit to Holt Warren's homestead were in full blaze, and the smoke was both white and black. A couple of riders had their backs to him and were watching.

Del held the horse still for a moment and took stock. Though the wind was not blowing, he could smell the odor of burning lumber, and bits of ashy debris floated on the air. The two riders were keeping an eye on the fire, but he thought he had a right to ask about it.

Del stood in the stirrups as his horse trotted to the scene. The rider on his left turned to look at him. Del did not know the man, but he thought he might be the stranger he had seen in the saloon on Sunday. His saddle had tapaderos.

The man on the right seemed familiar by way of his brown hat with a rounded crown. When he turned, Del recognized the insolent expression of Al Fisher.

Del nudged the bay in Fisher's direction and came to a stop a couple of yards away. The air was very dry and hot. "What's going on?" he asked.

"Doin' a little work."

"I can see that. What for?"

Fisher raised his chin. "I was told to."

"I guessed that. But why?"

"Keep out the criminal element. A place like this goes empty, and the crooks come in and use it to do their work. We'll come back tomorrow and take down the krells."

Del's blood rose. "It's not yours to burn or tear down."

Fisher shrugged. "I just take orders. But I don't think it was his, either. And it sure as hell ain't yours."

"Where's your boss?"

"He's at the home place, workin'. If he knew you was gonna come around snoopin', he might have come with us, just to knock you on your ass again."

Del glanced at the flames. They were burning bright orange but not leaping high. "I hope this doesn't get out of control."

"Hah. That's my worry."

"Yours and all the neighbors'."

"If we need you, we'll send for you. With a pigeon." Fisher spat to the side. "This is nothin'. Just burnin' a rat."

Overlin made his appearance as the men were drinking their coffee the next morning. The aroma of fried bacon hung in the

97

air, and Westfall was smoking a cigarette. The boss did not seem to be in a hurry, as he took off his hat, rubbed the tuft of hair on the top of his head, and put his hat on. He took in his hired hands with a sweeping glance.

He said, "Boys, I've got a job for all four of you. I want you to go to the other side of Coldwater Creek and push all of my stock about two miles north. There's pasture in there that hasn't been grazed much."

Macmillan said, "Do you mean where Holt Warren had his claim?"

"That would be the general area."

"I hope we don't run into trouble. Some of that is deeded."

"You won't. He never had a legitimate claim on that place anyway. There's a counterclaim filed on it right now." Overlin tightened his lips.

Macmillan looked at his coffee cup and returned to the boss. "They were burning down his buildings yesterday afternoon. I suppose you know that."

"I might have heard something about it." Overlin held his hand out like a fin. "But I'll tell you right now, men who work for me don't worry about what I know or don't know." Overlin addressed the others, with most of his attention directed toward Price and Westfall. "The Pyramid boys burned that place down to keep the rustlers from using it as a hangout. Somebody has to do something, and the Pyramid is losing stock just like we are. We can't have rustlers right there where we're going to run our cattle."

Del would have had a hard time phrasing a response even if he wanted to. It seemed to him that in addition to changing the sequence and thus the logic of events, Overlin was basing his version of things on an assumption that was far from being proved.

When the boss left, Del stole a glance at Macmillan. He knew he didn't have to say a thing. This was the way the big cattle-men had done it before, and they had gotten away with it, so Overlin and Hardesty were doing it now. Del thought it was a cold thing to do, running over the top of a small operator who couldn't defend himself anymore, as well as pushing up against others who had claims in the area.

From what he had observed, the grangers had not considered the aggression as something that was happening to them. Maybe they did not think there was much they could do about it except try to stay out of the way. But trouble might come their way after all. If it did, Del wondered how much some of them would resist.

Del tipped up his cup and finished his coffee. "I suppose we should get started."

Macmillan took out his tobacco and papers. "It's going to be a long day. Let me have a smoke first. Ed hasn't finished his yet, anyway."

CHAPTER SEVEN

Del took a chance and knocked on the back door of the ranch house. He did not know what the family's evening routine was, but he hoped Overlin was sitting in a stuffed chair in the front room, reading a cattlemen-controlled newspaper. For all he knew, the boss was still scowling over the exchange with Macmillan that morning.

Del knocked again and listened for footsteps. He thought he heard a light tread. The door opened, and Lawna faced him. He could not read anything definite in her expression.

She spoke in a low voice. "I can't see you right now. I can't talk to you."

"You can't talk to me at all?"

She frowned. "Not now."

"Well, I need to talk to you at some time. I—"

"Not now." Her voice was almost at a whisper.

"When?"

"Tomorrow at about this time. After you come in from your work."

"Where?"

"Down where you picked the chokecherries. I'll see you when you leave the barn, and then I'll go down there."

He took a breath. "All right." He was trying to think of what else he could say when she closed the door.

Clouds were moving in from the west as Del rode toward the

ranch after his day's work. Overlin had sent him and Macmillan to ride the range east of the ranch headquarters, and he was glad for the distance and solitude. All day long, he imagined what Lawna might say and what he would like to say, if he had a chance. He had two lines of inquiry for her—the urgent one, regarding how he stood with her, and the obscure one, entailing what she might know about her father's old friendship with Holt Warren. Sometimes all he could think about was Lawna and the golden swirl of their romantic moment, but at other times, he remembered that one reason he had stayed at the ranch this long was to learn something that might help set things right.

His calmer motive was not always foremost in his mind, and it remained vague because he did not know what there was to learn. But he was convinced there was something. It was a good rational line to follow, for his thoughts about Lawna always led him in a circle.

At present, the clouds were making him wonder whether he was going to be able to see her at all. They did not look like the quick, dark clouds that would dump a shower of rain or a torrent of hail and move on. Rather, they were dark grey, with a texture that reminded him of wet felt. He associated that appearance with moisture that rolled in, hung around, and gave things a slow soaking.

A light rain not much heavier than a mist was beginning to fall when he left the barn. He knew that if he listened to his own better judgment, he would stop at the bunkhouse for a coat or a slicker, but he did not want to see or talk to anyone. It would be better to show up later and give brief answers to any comments or questions.

Precipitation fell on the chokecherry leaves with a faint sound, not quite a patter. He stood among the bushes, but he did not have good shelter. Before long, drops were falling from the vegetation. If he touched a branch, the gathered water spilled from the leaves.

Daylight faded. His shirt was soaking up the moisture. His hat was wet, and water ran off the brim in little streams. The rain was now pattering on the leaves.

Muffled hoofbeats drew his attention. Two riders stopped at the ranch house. Rich Hardesty dismounted, and Al Fisher led his horse to the barn.

Del's hopes sank. He had to decide how much longer to stay where he was. He doubted that he could outwait Hardesty and still have a meeting with Lawna. He wondered if he should go to the bunkhouse now or wait to see what Fisher did.

Rain in itself did not bother him. He had seen plenty of it in Oregon. It did not go with a single kind of experience, but the hollow feeling he had now went with a cold rain. The gathering dusk and the misty atmosphere allowed him to see very little of the present scene, and his mind went back to another gloomy day.

He was eight years old. He had been living with his cousins ever since his mother left him with his father. His parents fought on days like this, when moisture collected on the inside of the windowpanes and ran down in streaks. He went with his mother, then back to his father, and on to his aunt and uncle and cousins. On a cold, rainy day, a woman came by. She stepped down from a shabby carriage, opened an umbrella, and walked to the door. She knocked and came in. Del did not recognize her. His cousins shouted, "Auntie Peg! Auntie Peg!" He realized that Peg was his mother's name. He did not know her in brown hair. She had colored it. When the cousins let her loose, she made her way to Del. She said she was leaving but would come back to see him. She never did. On a cold, rainy day in November, his aunt and uncle sat him down on a low stool in the kitchen and told him his mother had died in Seattle. He remembered the year, as he always did: 1885. He was eight.

Movement drew his attention to the barn. Fisher had come out. He pressed his hat on his head and made a direct line to the bunkhouse. Del figured he should now wait a little longer.

Fisher was standing by the cast-iron heating stove when Del entered the bunkhouse. No one paid Del much attention, as Fisher was holding the floor with a story. He ended it by saying, "And that was the last I seen of 'im."

Westfall, who did not often join in, went on to tell a story about a mule back home that showed up after being gone for more than a year. "Our guess was that someone swiped him, and he took that long to get away from 'em." The others paid attention to his story as Del hung his hat and changed his shirt.

"Hell, that's nothin'," said Fisher. "There's a true story about a horse down on the Red Desert, the other side of Rawlins, that's been loose and on the run for years. He had a saddle on him when he got away, and he's tried to get rid of it. He rubs it on rocks and knocks it against trees. He's worn the stirrups off and most of the other leather, so all he's got is the tree and the cinch. They see him out there, but no one can ever catch him."

Macmillan said, "Is the saddle still on his back?"

"I don't know. I haven't seen him myself."

"You'd think that after all this time, at some point, that saddle, or what's left of it, would have swung around and would be ridin' under his belly."

"I couldn't tell you."

"But you know it's a true story."

Fisher folded his arms. "It was told to me that way, by a fella who doesn't tell cock-and-bull stories."

The door opened, and Hardesty walked in with something of a swagger. The large rowels on his spurs made a clinking sound. He drew up next to Fisher and held his palms toward the heat. "Bill said for us to spend the night, so that's what we'll do. We'll go back in the morning unless it's still raining."

"This little rain won't last that long," said Fisher.

"You don't know."

Rucker spoke from the kitchen doorway. "You're just in time for supper. And in case anyone has forgotten, what I say goes, under this roof just like at the chuck wagon."

Fisher put on his vacant expression. "I never would have doubted it."

Del was glad to see Hardesty and Fisher leave when the morning showed blue sky. He wished he would see Lawna walk out into the sunlight, but she did not. He assumed he should wait for her again at the end of the day.

The ground was still soft as Del waited in the cool shadows of the evening. The red and yellow colors of sunset faded into the blue sky above. Birds twittered. From the peak of the barn, a dove called, "Hoo-hoo."

Del's pulse jumped at the sight of Lawna walking through the dusk. She had her blond hair tucked into the collar of a long, dark, lightweight coat, the kind that women wore when they traveled by train or stagecoach. She kept her hands in her coat pockets as she approached.

"Good evening," she said. "I'm sorry I didn't make it yesterday, but it wasn't possible, of course."

"Understood. I got wet, but nothing worse."

She huffed out a little breath. "Well, I know you wanted to talk to me."

He felt that he was starting from a dead stop. "I'm not very good at guessing games, and I didn't want to play one if I don't have to."

"You don't."

He had to work himself up again. "I don't want to make any

assumptions, or even any comments, but I guess what I would like to do is, well, know where I stand."

Her face did not have much expression, but it was not impassive. "I don't blame you. Sometimes things might seem as if they have more . . . importance than they do. Not that it wasn't important or didn't matter. It's just that there wasn't any kind of a . . . pledge involved in it."

He let out a breath. He thought maybe the worst was over. "That was one way I thought it might be."

"I don't mean to say that it didn't mean anything. But to be blunt, it doesn't mean that we're going to spend the rest of our lives together."

He felt a weight lifting. "I appreciate your being able to say that."

"I wouldn't want to string you along."

He saw the opportunity to try to be noble. "And I wouldn't want to say or do anything that would sully your chances with someone else."

She raised her eyebrows and tipped her head to one side. "I'm sure you never would. But don't worry about me in that respect. If anything, you've helped me. Being able to speak out loud to you has helped me see that I don't really intend to end up with him."

Or me, either. "I'm glad to hear it," he said.

She laughed. "And I'm sure you won't say anything to that effect, either."

He raised his hand as if he was swearing an oath. "I assure you."

"Thank you. You're a gentleman."

"I'm not, but thank you for saying it."

"Why not?"

"My understanding is that a gentleman comes from a certain

class of people and doesn't have to work for a living."

"There are different definitions," she said. "But we won't argue about it." She kept her hands in her pockets as she said, "Let's wish each other well."

"That's fine with me," he said.

Piano music, an indistinct singing voice, and laughter floated through the air in the Forge Saloon. An undercurrent of conversation and mild oaths flowed as well. Del stood near the bar, next to Macmillan. Price and Westfall had gone to congregate with the younger men their age.

Macmillan frowned. "Who's that fella with Al Fisher?"

Del did not turn to look, as he had seen them on the way in. "Someone new, I think. He was in here by himself last Sunday, and then I saw him with Fisher when they were burning down the buildings at that homestead." Del had to speak above the hubbub, and he did not want to say any names if he didn't have to.

"There's always one more, isn't there?" The first girl of the evening strolled by. "There's always one more of those, too."

Del did not know what he would do if he saw Maude. The girl who just passed by stirred no feeling in him, and he had had an emptiness since his disappointment with Lawna. He would just have to wait to see how he felt, but he told himself he had to be careful and resist impulses.

Del motioned with his thumb toward Fisher and the other man. "It doesn't surprise me to see those two. Hardesty was eating supper by himself in the café. I saw him when we rode in."

Macmillan said, "So did I."

Norris Drayton and Josh Crittenden made their way through the crowd and came to a stop. The old dentist was wearing his light tan summer jacket and pants with a white shirt, and his thinning white hair was clean. He smiled and said, "Another night out, eh?" His comrade was wearing the same grey suit as before and appeared to be in that early stage of the evening in which he did not say much. He touched his glasses and gave a brief smile.

"Looks like there's room to stand here," said Drayton. "Hope you don't mind."

"Not at all," said Del. He had the impression that Drayton would not mind continuing topics of conversation from before.

Crittenden, being a little closer to the bar, ordered drinks for the two of them. He handed a glass to his crony and mumbled a comment.

Another girl walked by, and Drayton raised his eyebrows. He lifted his head, as if to take in the perfume. "Ah," he said. "The memory is still there." As he took a drink, Del noticed the spots on the back of the old man's hand, which went with the redness at the sides of his nose.

Crittenden could just as well have seen a hand truck of bagged potatoes go by. He sipped from his drink, pressed his lips together, and stared at the empty space in front of him.

Del listened with half an ear to the piano player. The last three songs had all sounded the same as he banged them out, and the words were not distinguishable.

A rush of motion and voice brought him back to his group.

"Looks like the old liars' club is trying to take in younger members."

Malcolm Bain had made his appearance and was settling onto his cane. He was wearing his cap and a cloak, and he stood at full height with his shoulders squared.

Drayton said, "Good evening, constable."

Bain smiled and winked, and with a furtive move he must have seen on stage, he drew aside his cloak and revealed a brown shoulder holster with a black-handled piece that looked like a

.38 revolver. He smiled, showing a good set of teeth. "For the night shift."

"What's new?" Macmillan asked.

"Not much. Been following the Tom Horn case. He broke out a little while back, you know, but they put him right back in. He was supposed to be hanged back in January, but it was put off. He's got an appeal coming up, and if things go well, they'll hang him later in the fall."

Macmillan said, "It's a surprise he hasn't had his cattlemen friends get him off already. He's done a lot of work for them."

Bain smiled. "And all of it dirty. From what I heard, and you won't see this in the newspapers, they'd get him off if they wanted to. But they've gotten their use out of him, and he'd be a liability to them if he stayed around longer. He has too much on 'em."

Drayton said, "He won't peep, will he?"

"No, but he talks when he's drunk. I imagine he'll go game, not tell on anyone right up to the end, hopin' they'll get his sentence commuted after all." Bain raised his head. "I sure hope they don't. Even if he didn't kill that kid at Iron Mountain, which some people say he didn't, I think it would be a good ending if he was executed anyway, for all the other men he killed and was so proud of, doing his work for the bigwigs."

The piano player had stopped. Bain had been speaking above the noise, so he had an audience for his last two sentences.

"Thank you, thank you," said the piano player. He was standing and addressing the patrons. He was tall and slender, with close-set eyes and a narrow chest. "My name's Tom, and I'll be back to play a few more numbers for you." He waited for the light ripple of applause that followed. "And now, while I take my intermission, I believe someone else has a song to sing."

Tom stepped aside, and another man moved next to the

piano. He was of medium height and had a bushy white mustache.

"Thank you," he said. "I'm not a one-song man, but they told me I could have time for one song. I'm travelin' through, so any contributions will be appreciated. By the way, this is a song I wrote myself, and it's called 'Dark Sparrow Winter.' "

He sat down at the piano, thrummed the keys in a couple of different combinations, and began to play a sad melody. His voice was clear and strong as he sang the words.

Oh a cold wind blows tonight in wide Wyoming,
And a wet late winter snow lies on the ground.
I build up the fading fire at my hearthstone
And imagine what the spring will bring around.

It's been six long months since yellow leaves were
    falling,
And I chose to make my camp on higher ground
Here upon the southern slope of Sparrow
    Mountain
To forget about the girl who turned me down.

But the wind and snow of winter quite
    outmatched me,
And my horses disappeared one moonlit night,
Leaving tracks in crusted snow through crooked
    canyons
My two horses and a leader traveling light.

Through the maze of horse-thief trails on foot I
    tracked them
Till I came upon a camp at close of day.

In a shadowed rope corral among the cedars
Stood a dark horse with my sorrel and my bay.

At the fire sat a man, his pistol gleaming,
With his long hair like a horse thief or a tramp,
And he challenged me with words obscene and
    vulgar,
And demanded that I not approach his camp.

In a minute it was over, and the stranger
Was a lifeless form beside the flickering flame,
And the horses had stampeded, leaving nothing
But a killer and a victim with no name.

For a week I tracked those horses through the
    canyons
Till their trail led out upon the eastern plain
Where the snow from sun on rock and sage had
    melted,
And a dark cloud from the north brought snow
    again.

Back at home I tend the fire in my shanty
As I look upon the moonlight on the snow,
And I wonder if I'll ever find my horses
Or if the perfect truth I'll ever know.

    The man at the piano stood up and took off his hat, showing a balding head to go along with his white mustache. After the brief applause died away, he said, "Thank you. As I said before, I'm passing through. If you can help me on my way, I'd appreciate it." He handed his hat to the nearest man and walked away to stand at the far end of the bar.

As the hat went around the crowd, Del noticed that men were putting in nickels and dimes. He wondered if Fisher would contribute, but he did not see either of the two Pyramid hands. Conversations resumed, and the evening continued its flow.

The man named Tom returned to the piano and began playing a song that sounded like the ones he had played earlier. The two girls in bright outfits circulated in separate parts of the crowd. The hat came around, and Del put in a dime. The others in the group, including Malcolm Bain, chipped in as well.

Macmillan bought Malcolm Bain a drink. As before, the man in the cap and cloak said he could have only one, as he was on his way to work.

Drayton took a tan cigarette from his case and lit it. As he shook out the match, he said to Crittenden, "Tell them what you told me."

"I didn't tell you anything."

"About the trees."

"Oh, that's nothing."

Malcolm Bain said, "What about the trees?"

Crittenden pushed out his lips. "Nothin' to speak of. Just that the man I work for, who's got the mercantile, says he's goin' to sell trees next year. Says he'll have shade trees like elm and ash, and fruit trees like apples."

"That's good," said Bain, "to see more trees come to this part of the country."

Drayton said, "Men who plant trees have an eye to the future. Not just seein' how much money they can squeeze out of things at the present."

Bain took a sip from his drink. "Or what they can extract. You were in the extraction business, weren't you?"

The old dentist blew out a puff of smoke. "It was one thing I did. There wasn't much planting to do in that line of work, unless you consider dentures. Even then, they don't take root."

Crittenden said, "At least you didn't have to bury your mistakes. That's another kind of plantin'." He shook with mild laughter at his own joke.

Drayton twisted his mouth. "Where's he going to get those trees?"

"Where he gets everything. From his suppliers."

Del stepped back from the group to see if he could catch a glimpse of Fisher or his fellow rider. Del preferred to keep track of people he didn't trust, and he still did not see them.

A touch at his elbow brought him around. A pleasurable glow spread through him at the sight of Maude, attired in a low-cut, scarlet evening dress.

She touched her cheek and said, "How are you doing?"

His eyes took her in. "Pretty well, I think."

"Is there anything you'd like this evening?"

He spoke in a low voice. "Not right now. Maybe a little later, if the company thins out."

She touched his arm and held him with her softened hazel eyes. "Good enough. Maybe I'll see you later on." She exchanged greetings with Bain and Drayton and moved on.

Drayton moved to the bar and ordered drinks for himself and Crittenden. He stepped back into his previous spot as he handed a glass to his friend.

Crittenden opened his eyes but did not raise his eyelids all the way. "Another thing he says he might sell is bicycles."

"That's good," said Bain. "Bicycles and telephones help catch criminals." He tossed off the rest of his drink and said, "That's it for now. I'll see you all next time."

He made his halting way through the crowd, and the last that Del saw of him was when he reached the door.

A minute later, as Del was letting his eyes wander to see where Maude was, a gunshot sounded from outside.

Conversations changed to questions and answers. "What was that?" "Someone fired a shot." "Was it a rifle or a pistol?" "It sounded like a pistol to me."

The piano had gone silent, along with Tom's voice.

Men pushed toward the door, but no one went out. Someone said, "Get a lantern."

Del studied Macmillan's face. "Are you thinking what I am?"

Macmillan said, "He just left."

They pushed their way through the crowd and arrived at the door at the same time as a man with a lantern.

Outside, Macmillan pointed in the direction of the livery stable. "Let's try this way," he said.

Del's eyes adjusted as the men put the saloon behind them. A half-moon was out, so the night was not as dark as it seemed at first.

Ahead of them, in the middle of the street, lay a dark form. As they approached and the lantern light reached out, Del saw a pair of legs and the hem of a cloak. A couple of steps farther, the light showed on the face of Malcolm Bain and reflected on the gold chain that held the collar of his cloak. His eyes were closed, and blood leaked from the corner of his mouth. His cap lay in the street near his head. His right arm was stretched out, and just beyond his grasp lay his dark cane.

Several men were on their way from the saloon, muttering and exclaiming. The first ones passed the news back. Del heard the word "cripple."

Norris Drayton pushed up against Del on the left side. "It sure is," he said. "And he just left us. You wonder why in the hell someone would want to do something like that. What were we talking about? Trees. And bicycles. And before that, he went on for a little while about Tom Horn." Drayton's eyes moved to the small crowd and came back to Del and Macmillan. "That's not anything to shoot a man about, is it?"

Del shook his head. Bain had been much more vociferous the Sunday before.

Macmillan said, "I don't know what it was, but I'd bet a hat it wasn't anything he said tonight."

Del stood at the gate of the horse pasture, watching the animals graze. Here at the ranch, under a blue sky on a Sunday morning, the problems of town seemed far away. But he wondered how far they were. A week earlier, in his drunken rage, Malcolm Bain had ranted about hanging the ruling-class pigs from telegraph poles. Just before he died, he had made some casual comments about the bigwigs who had paid Tom Horn. But as Macmillan had suggested, talk of that nature did not give enough cause for a man to be shot in the street at night.

Del reviewed two things, more personal, that Malcolm Bain had said the week before. One was that Holt Warren was a good friend of his, and the other was that he knew what Bill Overlin did with Paul Gresham's Appaloosa horses. Del was not certain of the order of those two declarations, but he was pretty sure Bain had made both statements after the stranger came into the saloon.

Horses grazing in a pasture, a peaceful scene under a blue sky—Malcolm Bain would never see any of it again. Del wondered if the man carried a gun in a shoulder holster because of an imagined war with the ruling class or because of the danger of knowing details of other people's personal history. He did not think it was because of the dangers of working the night shift in the livery stable. He had interpreted Bain's comment to refer to his fanciful role of constable. But the gun itself was real.

Del's own words from an earlier day came back to him. He would not go along with something crooked. He had been convinced that Holt Warren's killing was crooked, but he did not have any more proof now than he did before. Still, he had stayed on at the ranch long enough. He knew where he stood with Lawna, and he did not think he would learn any more here about details from the past. If he went elsewhere, he might learn more. He knew what he had to do. He also had an awareness that this was a major moment in his life, one that would define him to himself if not to others.

He walked to the ranch house and knocked on the front door. Bill Overlin opened the door, looking a little plumper than usual in stocking feet and with no hat. His face was full and flush, while the top of his head where the tuft sprouted was paler.

"What do you need?" he asked.

Del had his sentence ready. "I've decided to ask for my time."

"Your time? You mean your pay?"

"Yes, sir."

"Then you're quitting?"

"Yes."

The boss narrowed his eyes. "Are you sure you want to do this? Because once you do, you can't change your mind."

"Yes, that's what I want."

"You want to quit."

"Yes, that's right."

The boss had his hand on the doorknob, and he made a hint of a motion of closing the door. "All right," he said. "I'll draw it up." He closed the door.

CHAPTER EIGHT

Del stopped to let his horse drink at Coldwater Creek. The evenings and mornings were cooler now in September, but the middle of the day warmed up as if summer days would never cease. In addition, the horse had to carry Del's duffel bag and bedroll as well as the rider, so a rest was in order. When Brush finished drinking, Del spurred him across the creek and swung his leg high to dismount.

Having crossed the creek at various points in the past couple of weeks, Del had a good sense of where he was. The Spoke lay behind him, straight south. If he were to follow the creek upstream around its northerly curve and go west, he would arrive at the Pyramid. If he went due north, he would find the charred remains of Holt Warren's place, and if he went east from there, he would come upon the whitewashed buildings of the Wiggins homestead. If he rode east from where he was now and crossed the creek to the south again, he would find himself in the town of Provenance.

The thought crossed his mind that he did not have to go anywhere, and of the five spots he reviewed on his mental map, he had seen enough of them for the time being. Sooner or later he would have to go somewhere, though, and Sunday was not a bad day for a social visit. Del cast an upward glance at the sun, checked his cinch, and swung aboard. Out of habit, he looked back at the site he was leaving, and he noted that the chokecherry leaves were turning color. Some had a light scarlet tinge, some were yellow, and some had fallen.

The white buildings sat undisturbed in the afternoon sunlight. Del guessed that he had missed the dinner hour, which he did not mind. A shiver ran through him at the memory of last Sunday's mutton stew. He slowed his horse to a walk as he approached the house, and he stopped at the hitching rail.

The door opened in the shade of the porch, and Wiggins stepped out in his side-to-side motion. He leaned forward in what Del interpreted as a gesture of humor and slapped the knee of his overalls.

"Hell's fire and little fishes! You're not movin' in, are you?"

"Not without an invitation." Sensing that his own humor went unrecognized, Del added, "No, it was not my intention. I have a place where I can stay." The green, scarlet, and yellow leaves appeared in his mind.

"Well, pile off, then, and come in and tell us all about it."

Del dismounted and tied his horse, then stepped up onto the porch and followed Wiggins into the house. He took off his hat. He expected to see company, so he was not surprised to find Homer Templeton sitting at the table. Behind the farmer, on the wall as before, hung the illustration of "The Angel in the House." Seeing it now for the second time, Del wondered if it represented something ideal for Wiggins or if it was just the kind of art he thought he should have on his wall.

Wiggins, wearing slippers, shuffled to his place at the head of the table and laid a hand on the back of the chair as he came to a stop.

He caught his breath and said, "Have a seat."

Del exchanged a greeting with Templeton and took a chair across from him.

Wiggins said, "Tell us what's new, then. I heard there was a shootin' in town. Fella got killed. The cripple that worked at the livery stable."

Del winced. "That's true," he said. "A shot in the dark. No witnesses."

"They say he was a friend of Holt Warren."

"That's what I heard."

Wiggins poked the tip of his tongue out between his lips and shook his head. "You wonder what he done."

"No one seems to know yet." Del noticed that each man had a glass of whiskey in front of him. He asked, "And how are you gentlemen?" As soon as he said it, he was aware of his use of the word.

Wiggins said, "Haven't made a million dollars yet today, but that's not unusual."

Templeton spoke in his deep voice. "No, it's not."

"And yourself?" said Wiggins. "Looks like you're on the move."

"I am. I gave up my job at the Spoke outfit."

Wiggins put his thumb and middle finger on his glass but did not raise it. "Hope there's no trouble."

"Well, there has been, though not for me. It started with the shooting of Holt Warren, and then they burned his place down."

Wiggins said, "I heard they didn't want rustlers staying there."

"I heard that, too, of course, and then this fellow was shot in town last night. I thought I had already put in enough time at the Spoke, so I decided to leave." Del wondered if Tess was in the kitchen and could hear him. His optimism sank when he realized that Clede might be there as well.

Wiggins rotated his glass. "What do you plan to do next?"

"Look for work."

"There's work to be found. Different kinds, dependin' on what a fella doesn't mind doin'."

"I'm not picky, though I don't care to work around hogs."

"Hah. I never liked it, either, but someone has to, and there's them that don't mind." Wiggins stared at his drink, and his eyebrows moved as if a thought had crossed his mind. "I don't have any work. Most of my land is leased out."

"I recall you saying something like that before."

"I'd go to town. That's where you find out about things. Say what you will, a saloon is not a bad place to hear about a job." Wiggins took a drink, held his glass in front of him, and tipped his head to the side. "Of course, it'll help a fella lose his job as well."

"I'll look around," Del said. "I thought I would drop by here and see if anyone knew of anything."

"Never hurts. We'll keep our ears open."

Del pushed his chair back. "I guess I'll be on my way, then." When no one spoke, he stood up.

"Come by any time," said Wiggins.

"Thanks." Del nodded to Templeton. As he turned to leave, Templeton's deep voice stopped him.

"You could come see me tomorrow. I might could use a hand for a day or two."

"Oh, that would be fine. How do I find your place?"

Templeton pointed with his thumb. "I'm straight east of here a mile. If you don't know whose fields you're goin' across, you might want to follow the section lines and go around."

"I'll do it that way. Thank you. I'll see you in the morning."

"Yup." Templeton lifted his glass about an inch off the table and paused.

Tess appeared in the doorway. She was wearing a grey apron over a dark blue dress, and her cheeks were flushed. In her hands she had a package wrapped in brown paper.

"Here's a small loaf of bread," she said. "I imagine you can use it if you're going to be staying on your own. It's not much."

He met her dark eyes. "Thank you."

"You're welcome." As she turned to go back to the kitchen, he saw that her dark hair was tied up in a red ribbon.

He said goodbye again to the two men and walked out.

Under the broad sky, with the sun still hanging high, Del did not have a plan for the rest of the day. He mounted his horse and rode out of the yard. For a lack of anywhere else to go, he decided to follow the section line south.

After half a mile, he came to a corner and turned left. He rode a mile east until he came to another corner. The road north would take him to Templeton's, but he did not need to go there now. The road south would take him toward town, but he did not need to go there, either, if he had work for the next day. But he had nothing to do where he was, in the middle of a wide, treeless grassland. He stopped to recover an earlier line of thought he had entertained.

Two questions persisted in his mind. One was whether Holt Warren was just a large inconvenience for the cattlemen who wanted to control the range or whether some other reason caused Overlin and Hardesty to make their move against him. A second question was why Malcolm Bain was killed on his way to work. Del recalled Norris Drayton saying that Maude knew Holt Warren as well as anyone did. She was also a friend of Malcolm Bain, as Del had observed. Until now, he had not thought of her after the shot was fired in the street. He was not stirred by the thought of physical closeness, but he was drawn by a sense that she had knowledge that mattered to him. He turned right and rode south toward Provenance.

The Forge Saloon had no other patrons when Del walked in from the bright afternoon. The piano had been pushed up against the wall, and chairs sat upside down on most of the tables. The only light came from two lamps hanging above the bar about twenty feet apart.

Mitchell stirred and moved into better light. "What'll it be today?" he asked.

"A glass of beer."

The bartender served it, and Del laid a dime on the bar.

Del said, "Quiet today."

"People stay home after trouble. You were here last night, weren't you?"

"Yes, I was. We left after the shooting."

"Just about everyone did. No one wants to stay around when a shot's been fired and they don't know who did it."

"I lost track of someone I was thinking of talking to later. That woman named Maude."

Mitchell's face showed no expression. "Oh, her. Yeah, she left, too. The fella that got killed was a friend of hers."

"That's what I understood." After a couple of seconds, Del said, "What would it take to find her at this time of day?"

Mitchell stared at him as if he had asked for whiskey before breakfast. "The girls sleep late, and even more so on Sundays. And they don't go out in public much, you know."

"I just wanted to talk to her, and there's not much going on in here."

"Just want to talk. That usually means that a man's stuck on a girl and she's trying to get rid of him."

"That's not the case here. I haven't known her long enough to get stuck on her, so she doesn't have a reason to want to get rid of me."

"Sometimes it takes only once. I've seen it."

"I don't think she even knows my name. But you can tell her who I was talking to last night, and I think she'll remember."

"Me tell her?"

"I can't very well go back there on my own."

"That's for sure." Mitchell stared through his spectacles. "You always want something, don't you?" He walked away, slipped past the end of the bar, and disappeared through the door near the anvil that decorated the wall.

Mitchell returned a couple of minutes later and stayed at the far end of the bar, polishing drink glasses.

Del made his beer last, but he finished it and ordered another before the door at the back opened. His pulse jumped as a woman walked into the dim light.

She was not dressed for the night, and she did not swing her hips as she approached him. Still, she was wearing a low-cut apricot-colored dress, had her hair combed, and had taken the time to put shadow on her eyes and rouge on her cheeks.

"I thought it was you," she said. "What do you have in mind?"

"I just wanted to talk."

She frowned. "That's what he said. I don't know what we have to talk about."

His eyes drifted over her. She had a subdued air about her, with a soft shine in her hazel eyes. He wondered if she had been crying, which would have been normal with the loss of her friend, and he wondered if she had braced herself up for a pos-sible work engagement. He had told himself earlier that he did not have a physical interest in her today, and he did not feel any spark of desire, yet he felt something like a glow emanating from her—the combination of her womanness and of her being a complete human being and not just a woman of the night.

She must have felt his eyes on her, for she said, "Do you want to go to the room?"

"No," he said, trying to withdraw his attention, but admitting to himself that the thought was not very far away. He had a line prepared, and he heard himself deliver it. "I would like to give you a token of my esteem." He handed her a silver dollar.

She pushed his hand toward him. "I don't need your money," she said. "Not a handout."

He knew he had made a mistake. He had wanted to be generous, and even as he saw her as a real human being, he had followed the easy assumption that people in the world of night life and servitude responded to money like horses and dogs responded to food. "I'm sorry," he said.

She narrowed her eyes. "I still don't know what you want."

He had another line prepared. "I would like to learn a few things about what has happened in and around the town."

Her gaze relaxed, but she continued studying him. "It depends on what you want to know. I'm not going to be someone's paid stool pigeon."

"I'm sorry. That was my mistake. I know you're better than that."

She smiled. "You think you know me. At the same time, you act like you're afraid of me. Too bad you don't want to go to the room. Your fear would melt away."

He felt a wave go through him. "I know. But standing by the fire is a pleasure in itself. And I'm not so afraid of you. Actually, I trust you. And that's why I want to talk to you. Can I buy you a drink?"

"Just one."

They sat at the shadowy edge of the room, near the wall opposite the bar, not far from the mute piano. An awareness went through Del that just the night before, Malcolm Bain had stood in this saloon and joked about being a constable, and a week before, on an empty Sunday afternoon, he had told bits of his life story while railing about the unfairness of life.

"Go ahead," she said.

He met her eyes and did not find any resistance. "To begin with, I want to say how sorry I am about what happened to your friend last night. I didn't know him very well myself, as I met him in here on only three occasions, but I could see that you were friends."

"Not everyone liked him. He tended to speak his mind. But,

123

yes, we were friends. We had things in common. I wouldn't say we were outcasts, but we lived somewhat in the same level of society, if you want to call it that. You know what I mean. You cowpunchers and farm hands have your own level."

Del thought of Clede and did not like to be grouped with him, but he realized he was going to work for a farmer in the morning. "As far as that goes, I've left the ranch where I was working. But I know what you mean." She did not say anything in response, so he continued. "One of the reasons I left was that I was troubled by what happened here in town last night. Other things had gone on that I thought were wrong. I didn't know for sure that this was related, but I thought it was time for me to go. So I quit."

"You worked for Bill Overlin, didn't you?"

"Yes, I did. But rest assured that I don't owe him any loyalty."

She shrugged.

"And I hoped you could help me understand if there's a connection."

She sat back and folded her hands on the table in front of her. "I can tell you what I know for sure, but it's not much. Anything else would be what I heard."

"Let me start with this question. I was in here a week ago, on Sunday afternoon, and our late friend had been up all night, so he was, you might say, free with his words."

"He had that tendency."

"And one thing he made a remark about was some Appaloosa horses."

She made a small wave with her hand. "That's an old story."

"So I gathered. But I don't know what's behind it." When she didn't budge, he said, "I'm talking about some horses that belonged to Paul Gresham, of course."

"I know that. But I don't know what you're getting at."

"I don't know what the real story is. At the ranch, they'll say

Overlin sold the horses, but our friend said he knew what really happened."

Maude relaxed her shoulders and put both hands on her glass. She seemed to study the surface of her drink as she began to speak. "This was before I came here, but I've heard the story more than once. Paul Gresham had a fancy for Appaloosa horses, and he had a couple that he was quite proud of. When he died and Bill Overlin took over his place, Bill got rid of the horses. You know, some cattlemen, and horse breeders, have a prejudice against Appaloosas. Consider them an inferior breed. So Bill got rid of them."

"Sold them?"

She raised her eyes to meet his. "That was the story. He said he sold them to a horse buyer who was buying up horses for someone else's war, some country in Europe, where only one out of ten horses made it to the battlefield." She paused. "That's what he said, and it was enough for some people to be bitter. But Holt Warren said that he had it on good authority that Overlin had his hired man at the time take the Appaloosas out to a place where they took their cull horses, and he shot them."

"Because he wanted to rub out any traces of Paul Gresham."

"That's the conclusion to either version of the story, but if the more spiteful version is true, you can see why he wanted to keep it a secret."

"But Holt Warren knew it, or at least knew of it."

She nodded. "Yes. That's the nature of secrets."

"And Malcolm Bain, being Holt Warren's friend, knew it, too."

"Yes. They had a good level of confidence."

Del shook his head. "It's believable, but it doesn't seem like enough reason for someone to take action against a small-time cattleman. And the accusations about branding and brand-changing didn't seem to have much of a base."

Maude took a sip of her drink. "It all goes back a long way."

"Before the horses?"

"Yes. And like I say, it was before I came here. So the story is just something I heard, and some of the people are just names to me."

Del decided to help her along. "I've heard some of the story myself, about the group of friends. There were four at first, and then Bill Overlin worked his way in, and then there were two couples, and Holt Warren was left on the outside."

"That's how I heard it. Everyone loved Diana, but Paul married her. And Bill married Imogene."

"I can't help sympathize with Holt Warren."

Maude's face had a faint glow, as of reminiscence. "He took it as well as he could, and I don't think he ever did anything malicious."

"You mean by inventing stories to tell his friends, like you or Malcolm Bain?"

"Yes, or earlier, by telling Diana. But he also remained friends with Imogene. I believe he lost communication with Diana, but Imogene wrote to him."

"And they were just friends, weren't they?"

"Correct. But being good friends, Holt tried to discourage her from marrying Bill, said he was a bad egg. After she was into the marriage for a while, she began to notice things. When she had a few added up, she told Holt about it in a letter."

"Oh. So it wasn't the kind of letter that a bride writes to her friends about life on the ranch."

"No. It was not meant to be passed around. They had always been frank with one another, and she had things to express."

Del glanced over his shoulder to make sure no one else had come in, although he had not seen the door open. The only other person present was Mitchell, who kept his distance at the far end of the bar.

Maude resumed in a low voice. "Imogene confided to Holt that she thought Bill had had an interest in Diana all along. She felt that she was a second choice, and even though she was going to have a baby, things were not getting better. Winter set in. Paul, as you may have heard, was caught in a snowstorm in the canyon and died."

"Yes, I've heard that."

Still in a low voice, cautious and deliberate in her enunciation, Maude continued. "Imogene said that she thought Bill might have had something to do with Paul dying, but she didn't have anything definite. Holt thought that the winter might be getting to her, and her state of expecting a baby might have led her to have strange thoughts. Then she wrote him another letter, saying some of the same general things she said before, but also saying she didn't trust Bill. She had 'premonitions' about him and didn't like to have him stand in back of her, especially now, in the condition she was in, when she couldn't move around very fast."

"Whew."

"Holt said he didn't know how much to believe and how much of it might have come out of some melodrama or dime novel. And then she died."

"And he had the letters."

"That's right. But it was all hearsay. He hung onto them in case anything ever came up where they might be useful."

Del remembered his beer and took a drink. "And so," he said, "do you think that at some point, someone else got a hint that those letters existed?"

Maude renewed the lower tone of her voice. "I think that may have happened, though I don't have an idea of what happened first. At some point, Holt decided that he shouldn't be the only one to have this knowledge, so he shared it with Malcolm Bain."

"Oh, my God."

"I know. But Holt did not want the information to end with him. He may have already feared for his life. Malcolm had been a friend of Paul Gresham as well, and he and Holt held a great many things in confidence."

Del said, "Malcolm may have been discreet when he was sober, but I heard him blab something in here just last week about the Appaloosa horses. He may have let things slip at other times."

"That's why I said I didn't know at what point Holt told Malcolm. Just like I don't know at what point Bill Overlin started his campaign. He may have built up the story about rustling so he would have a reason to go after Holt, but he may have started it sooner, for the usual reasons that people talk about—to control the range for themselves and to run off others when they can. And that could be when Holt got worried and told his story to Malcolm."

"Either sequence is reasonable." Del glanced around before mentioning another name. "I still wonder why Hardesty would play in. He's the foreman of the Pyramid."

"I know who he is. And I would say he might have a couple of reasons. The rustler story is convenient for him because it might make it seem as if he is running the ranch better than he is, as the rustling would cause him to be suffering losses against his good management. The other motive would be to stay on good terms with his future father-in-law. And then there's the general reason I just mentioned with Overlin—to control things."

Del raised his eyebrows. "You have a pretty good view of circumstances for a girl who doesn't go anywhere."

She blinked her eyes and looked straight at him. "Holt Warren was a good friend of mine. Malcolm Bain was a friend, too, but to a lesser extent. And I hear a great deal of talk in here."

Del came back to the original thread. "And so there were two letters?"

"There may well have been more, but two of them could have been damaging."

"Does anyone know where those letters are now?"

Maude shook her head. "I would expect them to be hidden in a good place, so I imagine they have gone up in smoke."

Del was letting his horse drink from the town water trough when Macmillan came in from the south, riding the long-legged pale horse from his string. He stopped at the trough, dismounted, and let the horse drink.

"Afternoon," he said.

Del returned the greeting.

Macmillan was dressed as usual, in his dust-colored hat, grey shirt, brown cloth vest, denim trousers, and spurred boots. He took off his hat and set it on the saddle horn. As he leaned to splash his face in the water, the bald spot showed on the back of his head. He stood up straight, blew a spray of water from his mouth and mustache, and wiped his face with his hands.

"That felt good," he said.

"Looks like it."

"I didn't know if I would find you here. You left before I had a chance to talk to you by yourself."

Del shrugged. "If I had known, I could have stayed a little longer."

"It's just as well. I felt like gettin' away anyway." Macmillan's gaze went up and down the street. "I don't feel good at all about what happened last night. He was a friend of mine, of sorts."

"I didn't know him, just met him a couple or three times, but he didn't seem so bad."

Macmillan put on his hat. "Have you heard anything more

about why someone would want to shoot him?"

"Not much. I was in the saloon for a little while and talked to that woman named Maude. She was a friend of his, too."

"Oh, yeah. I know who you mean."

"She mentioned things that most people already know—that Malcolm Bain was friends with Holt Warren, and they both knew Bill Overlin from earlier times."

"Yeah. I know all of that."

"And the story of how Bill sold Paul Gresham's Appaloosa horses."

"I've heard that, too."

Del frowned. "What's the trouble with Appaloosas, anyway? What do people have against them?"

"Oh, it's like people say about Arabians and other breeds, that they're nervous, spooky, stubborn, hard to train. People have got similar prejudices against pintos. A good part of the time, they make a general judgment based on only one horse, that they may not be good at handling. Or just as often, they repeat what they've heard. Some men even have prejudices against palominos, or horses with light-colored hooves." Macmillan pointed with his thumb over his shoulder. "Is there anyone in the saloon now?"

"There wasn't when I left a few minutes ago."

"I thought I might drop in. Are you on your way somewhere?"

"Not in a hurry, but I think I've had enough for the day. I've got some work lined up for tomorrow. Farm work."

"Oh. Then you haven't wasted time."

Del smiled. "I don't know."

"I don't blame you for leaving the Spoke."

"I had enough, I guess. It just seemed like it was time to go."

"Rucker said the boss let on that you left because you couldn't get anywhere with the girl."

"I wonder if he believes it. But it's as good a story as any."

CHAPTER NINE

Del sat on his bedroll in the grey light of morning and ate the second half of the small loaf of bread. Moments from the day before came to him, including his conversation with Macmillan. He felt guilty for not having told his fellow puncher what he knew, after Macmillan had been forthright about what he thought about the cattlemen's motives. On the other hand, Del recognized the possibility that two men had been killed for knowing too much, so he was not in a hurry to share information he had just heard. Perhaps with a little time, he would have a better idea of how valid or pertinent it was. He could share his impressions with Macmillan later.

A fringe of sunshine was showing in the east when he saddled his horse, tied on his bedroll and duffel bag, and led his horse away from the quiet campsite. He put his foot in the stirrup and swung his leg high in order to mount up.

Sunlight was spreading onto the side of the house and the barn when he rode into Templeton's yard. Traces of paint showed on the weathered lumber. Del could not guess the age of the buildings, as the cold, dry winters and the wind at all seasons could make a two-year-old structure look twenty. Two elm trees, about fifteen feet tall and thirty feet apart, had meager foliage, and the slender branches carried scars from the hail of some previous year.

A whiff of woodsmoke and a wisp of white told him that someone had a cookstove going. Half a dozen brown and white chickens scratched and clucked in the sparse weeds near the barn. The clucking became a little louder as he swung down from his horse, and the barn door opened.

Homer Templeton appeared with a pitchfork in his hand. He wore a flat-brimmed, flat-crowned brown hat with a hole in the ridge of the crown. His face lay in shadow, but Del knew him by his tall and slender build, his jug ears, and his large hands. He was wearing a coarse grey work shirt, brown suspenders, denim trousers with folded cuffs, and brogan shoes. His pants had dirt on the knees. With his free hand he took a cigar from his mouth, and his deep voice carried.

"You made it."

"Yes, I did."

"You can put your stuff in the barn and your horse in a pen, and we'll get you started."

Templeton was waiting for him when he stopped out into the yard. The farmer no longer had his cigar and was holding a field hoe with its head down and the pitchfork with its head up. He handed the hoe to Del. "Take this."

He led the way out of the barnyard and followed a narrow path north through a close-cropped pasture. The land dipped down, and they continued walking. Templeton stooped and crawled through a three-wire fence to a second pasture, where a couple of bony-hipped brindle cows were grazing. Del followed.

The farmer led him to a low spot along the west edge of the pasture, where dull green vegetation spread over an oval-shaped area about twenty yards wide and forty yards long.

"Here," he said in his deep voice as he came to a stop. "This patch gets bigger every year, and I'm tryin' to fight it." He poked with the tines of his pitchfork. "Nettles mostly, and some thistles. What I need you to do is cut 'em all out and pile 'em in the lowest spot over there by the fence. There's kind of a hole there. You'll see where I piled 'em in the past." He raised his large hand and made a sideways motion. "You want to cut them below the surface of the ground, or you won't do any good. I try to get at these earlier in the year, but I had too much to do. So the ground's dry, and the stems might be tough, but I want you to get 'em out the best you can."

Del surveyed the sea of weeds. "I'll do my best. Once I've cut them, how do you want me to carry them to the pile?"

"Oh, I'll leave you this." Templeton handed him the pitchfork.

Not a breath of air stirred in the low spot as Del worked through the morning. This was the dream of many people, he thought, to have their own land under the open sky. He would like to do that himself someday, and he wasn't afraid of brute labor like this. But it was good to be reminded that if a fellow had his own place, every task was his. He could pick his jobs, but the ones he put off would always be staring him in the face. Not everyone did things the same, of course. Some men let weeds grow and junk pile up. Others kept their places neat as a pin, and then they died or sold out, and all their tidy work was good only for the time they were able to keep it up. Or others came and shot a man down and burned him out.

Del shook his head and went back to the positive thoughts. A man tried for as long as he could, and the effort was worth it in itself. He worked for what he got, he earned his own way, and he didn't cheat or bully. And when time passed him by, maybe someone would draw water from a well he put in, sit in the shade of a tree he planted and watered, or graze animals in a pasture he tried to keep clean. Then again, someone might come and take his family, tear down his buildings, and cull his horses.

He tried again to think of things more positive, like a dark-haired girl who gave him a loaf of bread, but he did not have much to go on. More familiar images crowded in, such as waiting in the rain, or waiting again for a blond-haired girl in a long coat who didn't take her hands out of her pockets, or sitting in a dim light talking in hushed tones to a hazel-eyed woman who worked her way through life and saw her friends rubbed out for no good reason.

At midday, he walked up to the house. He had not had a drink of water all morning, and he had sweated plenty. He found the pump, and after washing his face, he brought up cooler water to drink.

Footsteps sounded, followed by Templeton's deep voice. "I was about ready to go git you. It's time for the dinner bell. My wife should bring somethin' out in a short while."

Del stood up and put on his hat. "That sounds good."

The boss's Adam's apple went up and down. "How's the work goin'?"

Del shrugged. "All right, I guess. Like you said, the ground's hard, and the stems are tough, but I whale away. The handle of that hoe is kind of short and has some give to it. You know, it tapers at the end and has a curve in it, so I've had to learn to aim it."

"It's what I've got. The first handle was of pine, though it was supposed to be of ash, when I bought it back in Indiana. It splintered on me, so I had to make this one. Out of chokecherry. It's not as easy as you think. First, you need to find a trunk that's thick enough and straight enough for more than four feet. Five feet is better. Then you don't want to peel it right away, or it'll split when it dries. So you let it sit for a year, and then the skin is harder to get off. You need a strong knife and a rasp like you use on horse hooves. Not only do you have to get off all the old, tight bark, but you have to rasp off all the knots. That's the one I'm workin' on now, when I can find time. Meanwhile, you make do with what you've got."

Del had heard the expression before. He said, "Oh, it works."

"Sure it does. Here's Emily."

A short, round woman in a bonnet and a grey kitchen dress was carrying a faded wooden tray and taking small steps. As she approached, Del saw a wide crockery bowl full of white beans and bits of ham. He smiled, but she did not look at him. She was keeping an eye on the bowl.

"Thank you," he said as she handed him the tray. He observed her pale blue eyes and mouse-colored hair, and still she did not look at him.

"Welcome," she said. Her glance flickered to him and away. She said to her husband, "I can use more spuds whenever you can dig 'em."

"Yum, uh-huh," he said, in his deep voice. Then to Del, "I'll leave you to it. You might want to take some water with you in the afternoon."

"It occurred to me. I've got a canteen."

"Seen that."

Del piled the last of the nettles and thistles in the late afternoon. He wondered what his next job would be, if there was one. Templeton had spoken of a couple of days of work, and he should have estimated about a day for the weed patch.

Del left the hoe and pitchfork by the barn door. As he was washing up at the pump, Templeton appeared again.

"You can put up in the barn tonight," he said. "The wife'll have supper for you in a little while, and breakfast in the morning as well. We feed you."

Mrs. Templeton brought him a large bowl of beef stew, along with two slices of heavy brown bread and two little crockery jam pots. She did not look at him for more than a second at a time, but she did speak. She said that the potatoes, carrots, and onions in the stew all came from her garden, as did the rhubarb and the gooseberries in the two little pots.

He ate his meal. He thought the stew had more than enough

salt, and the two preserves were sour from lack of sugar, but it was all much better than the mutton stew that lingered in his memory.

At dusk, as Del sat in the shade of the barn, a man walked into the yard and knocked on the farmhouse door. Even in the fading light, Del was sure it was the man he had seen in the saloon and later with Al Fisher. He was dressed in his common work clothes and seemed to be traveling on foot.

Templeton came to the door and had a brief exchange with the man, with their voices going up and down. The farmer closed the door, and the visitor walked away.

Ten minutes later, Templeton came out of the house and found Del. He kept his deep voice at a low level.

"Don't know if you saw that fella that came by."

"I was sitting right here."

"He was lookin' for work. I told him I didn't have any. I didn't invite him to say. Some people would, but we've already got company. I believe he was on foot."

"Seemed to be. I imagined he left his bag out at the edge of the yard."

"May have. I don't think he's up to anything, but I thought I'd mention it. In case you hear somethin' in the night."

"I'll have it in mind."

Templeton brought a stack of three hotcakes and a small jar of molasses for breakfast. On a second trip, he carried a coffeepot and a cup. He poured a cupful and took the pot inside the house. As with the previous meals, Del sat on the ground in front of the barn and ate his food.

The hotcakes were heavy but cooked all the way through. The molasses had a bitter taste but added flavor. Del recalled the boss's words from the evening before. "We feed you."

When Del was finished, Templeton came out of the house

wearing his hat. Del figured it was time to go to work, so he stood up.

Templeton came to a stop. He had a lit cigar in his hand. He took a puff, blew the smoke away, and spoke in his deep voice. "I work a deal with my neighbor. We trade work. I help him, and he helps me. So I'm sendin' you over in my place today. You're still workin' for me, but you'll be doin' the work for him."

"I understand."

"His name's Jasper. He's got all girls. Four of 'em. They're good at milkin' cows, tendin' to the big garden, and makin' butter, but he needs a cellar dug. He's got a hired man that helps with the cattle and the hay equipment and whatnot, but he needs another hand to help the hired man with diggin' a root cellar. For potatoes, turnips, and punkins."

Del could see the logic. Jasper wanted to collect on some work that was due him, and it was worth Templeton's while to pay someone else who was suited for that kind of labor. Del said, "Should I ride over there, then, and leave my things here?"

"Yup. That's the idea."

"And how do I find his place?"

"Go south on the section line here till you come to the corner, and he's on the right."

"Then I've ridden past it."

"Sure you have. He's easy to find. And they've got wash hangin' out almost every day, not just on Monday. Don't worry about the girls, though. They won't distract you. They do their work, and none of 'em's pretty at all."

Del found the Jasper homestead where he expected. Bright white articles were flapping on the clothesline, but he did not have to avert his eyes, as the items proved to be sheets and pillowcases.

He wondered if, by the oddest chance, he would end up working with the man who had knocked on Templeton's door. He assumed it would not be the case, as Templeton said that Jasper kept a hired man. Del also reasoned that the traveler would have stopped at Jasper's first, and if he had been hired, he would not have gone on to Templeton's. So Del rode north up the lane to the yard with no preconceptions of what anyone would look like, except that the farmer's daughters would not be lovely mermaids.

The barnyard came alive as Del rode the last fifty yards. Sheep bleated, and calves bawled. Hogs grunted. The hooves of a larger animal thumped on a corral plank. A flock of white, grey, and brown chickens cackled and dithered, and a pair of large grey geese with thick orange beaks came hissing as he stopped in the yard.

The barn sat on the west side of the yard, good for blocking wind and giving afternoon shade. Lower buildings faced the yard from the north side, and the house lay on the east, or right, side.

A red-haired man came out of the house, putting on a pale green cloth cap. He had a large upper body, with a broad abdomen and thick arms. He wore a tan shirt and matching pants of light canvas, with dark green suspenders. He brushed off his mouth and smiled.

"How do you do?" he asked.

"Fine, thanks. I'm here for Homer Templeton."

"I thought so. I'm J.M. Jasper. Go ahead and get down."

Del dismounted and stood with his reins in hand. "My name's Del Rowland."

Jasper stood close as he shook hands and released. He was clean-shaven with bright blue eyes that took a quick measure of his new worker. "I'll tell you what I've got to do. I have a root cellar laid out, and my hired man knows how I want to have it done. You can work alongside him. You look like a cowpuncher. You're not afraid of a shovel, are you?"

"Not at all."

"Good. I'll introduce you to my hired man. We just finished milking, and he's cleaning up. Tie your horse here."

Del tied his horse and followed Jasper into the barn, where a row of a half-dozen stanchions was built along the back wall. The smell of cattle hung in the air, and a stout man in a battered hat was shoveling fresh manure into a wheelbarrow.

The boss spoke a word that Del didn't catch, and the workman turned around. Del recognized him as the short-faced man who had been playing solitaire in the saloon. The name came to mind. Simms.

"Gil," said the boss, "this is your helper."

Simms smiled as he held out a thick hand. "I think we've met. Gil Simms."

"We have. Del Rowland."

Jasper spoke again. "I'll show him where to put his horse, and you can get started."

"Sure. I'll be done here in a minute."

Del put his horse in a pen and waited in the barnyard. Simms came out and led him to the excavation site, which was near the northeast corner of the house. A rectangle about ten feet by twelve had been cut out of the shortgrass sod.

"This is it," said the hired man. "We'll go get some tools."

Simms led the way back to the barn, where he handed Del two shovels, a pick, and a digging bar. "I'll get the wheelbarrow," he said. He returned with the wooden wheelbarrow he had been using earlier. It had been emptied but not washed, and a film of fresh residue was drying. With the tools loaded, Simms picked up the handles and wheeled the vehicle to the site of the cellar.

A half-smile spread on his short face, creasing his eyes.

"Pretty simple. We're gonna dig about four feet down. Then they'll build the walls up about two feet high all around, a foot or so back from the edge. Then they put on a roof. We want to throw this dirt back about three or four feet around so we don't have to move it twice. It'll go back up against the walls before everything's done." He took in a deep breath and let it out. "I think it would be good if we work one on a side. You throw the dirt one way, and I throw it the other. What do you think?"

"Sounds reasonable."

"Do you shovel to the right or to the left?"

"I haven't thought about it. Either way, I guess."

"Good. I shovel to the left. So you can work on the right side."

The two men dug away. Simms was a steady worker, but he was also a steady talker. He had spent a good part of his life driving freight wagons and delivery wagons. It was the work he liked best. He had worked in a slaughterhouse and an icehouse, and everyone did farm work at one time or another. More beef cows than milk cows out here, but Jasper had half a dozen milk cows. The girls did the milking, morning and night. Out here, everyone had brands on their cattle. Seemed like a big item. Jasper didn't have a brand. The big men made it hard for the little men to register a brand.

About a foot down, they hit harder digging. The greyish-brown topsoil gave way to a light tan clay. Del used the digging bar, and Simms used the pick. The two methods loosened the dirt about the same.

When they were shoveling again, Simms came around to the topic of women. He didn't have any trouble with women. That was the kind of trouble he would like to have, some woman pushing him to be successful. Maybe it would help him have his own place, or his own business. And like a lot of fellas, he'd like to have a woman and a house to come home to, a pup on the rug at some point. Of course, not all women were fertile. Templeton's wife might be barren. Not Jasper's, though. The girls were all homely, like goslings that hadn't gotten their feathers yet, but that was not a bad quality. Not everyone could be a princess like the one they said the Pyramid foreman was all het up about.

The two workers set aside their shovels and loosened up more dirt. Simms put a pinch of tobacco in his mouth and was ready to go again. As he flung dirt, he returned to the topic of women. There was someone for everyone. You just had to meet 'em. He had a girl once who was going to marry him, but she left him. He couldn't blame her. He got into a jam when he ran over a little boy with a freight wagon. It was dark and storming, no time for some kid to be out on the streets, but they were able to prove he'd been drinking, so the boss fired him, the girl didn't want to have anything to do with him, and he was knocked flat. But he got back on his feet, like he always did.

Simms pushed the head of his shovel into the lower ground in front of him and leaned the crook of his elbow on the tip of the handle. "Everyone gets a second chance. Not only to make your own fortune, but to meet your better half. I believe that. And I believe what they say, that no matter who you are, there's someone out there for you."

Del did not think that Josh Crittenden would agree, and he wondered about Holt Warren and Malcolm Bain.

Simms spat across his elbow. "Just be realistic. If you don't look like a Greek god, you're not gonna get a goddess."

Del said, "Not to change the subject, but did a fellow come by yesterday evening, looking for work?"

"Yes, he did. Said he'd been punchin' cows for the Pyramid, and they didn't have any more work for him."

"That's who I thought it was, but he burned buildings as much as he punched cows. He went to work for the Pyramid after that other fellow named Lee Hilton, the one who shot Holt Warren, was working there."

"Oh, I heard about that. They say he went away."

"Maybe he came back, and that's why this fellow is out of work."

"I don't know why he'd come back, but I don't keep track of them. Doesn't put anything in my pocket."

Del admired the finished excavation with its squared sides and level floor. A great deal of dirt had come out of the hole, and it grew as it piled up. After about two feet of clayish soil, the ground had become softer again, though it did not change much in color. The easier digging had come at a good time, as the sun had moved over to the latter part of the afternoon.

Jasper approached his two workers as they were on the way to the barn with the tools. He said to Del, "You've got a horse. How would you like to go out and bring in a cow for me?"

"I suppose I could."

Jasper turned to Simms. "Gil, you can go with him. Take the dark horse. He shouldn't give you any trouble. Use the saddle you used the other time."

Simms gave his half-smile. "What's it look like?"

"It's a brown cow, half Jersey. Not a real big one."

Simms did not show any recognition.

Jasper said, "You can tell a Jersey. They're a pretty color of brown, and they've got big, round eyes." He turned to Del. "Do you know what I mean?"

"I have a general idea of what a milk cow looks like, as opposed to a beef cow. And I assume this one doesn't have a brand."

"That's right."

"Which way do you think it went?"

"I believe it got through the fence on the south side. It's not the first time. They head for the creek. It's as if they can smell a mudhole from miles away."

"We'll look for her."

Del and Simms rode down the lane, away from the house. Simms did not look like a natural rider, but he stayed in the saddle well enough.

Del said, "So you don't have a good picture of this cow or what she looks like."

"Not to speak of. The girls know 'em all by name and take 'em in and out, but all I ever see is their hind ends. You give me a draft animal, to pull a wagon or a mowin' machine, and that's different."

"I thought milk cows came in at the end of the day to be milked, but I've heard of some that liked to hide out or go their own way, especially if they're going dry."

"That's cows."

"Range cattle are a lot harder to find. You can scour an area with four or five riders and think you got everything, come up short on your count, and go back the next day and find two or three pairs that slipped through."

They rode south of the farm a little over a mile, and Del saw a speck in the west. He said, "That looks like a brown cow, but I'd have to get a lot closer to see if it could be the one. Can you lope?"

"Oh, yeah."

"Let's go, then." Del touched a spur to Brush, and the sorrel broke into a lope. The dark horse followed and kept up, with Simms clutching the reins and hanging onto the saddle horn as he bobbed up and down.

Three-quarters of a mile later, they slowed to approach the cow. Del rode wide to each side and did not see a brand, so he took down his rope. Simms's horse had slowed to a jolting trot, and now the pug-like rider had pulled the dark horse to a walk.

The cow was moving at a fast walk, about ten yards ahead.

"Do you think this is the one?" Del asked.

"I think it might be, but I can't be sure."

"Well, she's brown, but I don't know Jerseys all that well, and she doesn't have much of a bag like she should have at this time of the day."

"Unless she's goin' dry, like you said."

"That's true. And a range cow with any bag at all would have a calf with her. Let me ride ahead and get a better look." Del gave a kick, and Brush shot ahead, then turned as Del tried to stop the cow. He had his coiled rope in his right hand but had not built a loop.

Out of the rolling landscape appeared two riders. Del recognized them as he saw them—Fisher and Hardesty. Del was confident they were all on public land, near the area where Overlin had pushed his cattle. The Pyramid was farther west, but Hardesty made free with the land over this way as well.

Del stopped and waited, and the cow got away. Simms stopped as well.

Hardesty fired a shot in the air. He and his rider came straight on at a run, then stopped in a scramble of hooves and a small cloud of debris.

Hardesty barked, "What in the hell do you think you're doing?"

Del put his hands on his saddle horn. "Looking at a cow."

"You've got your rope out. You were about to brand that cow."

"Not by a long shot. I'm doing a little work for J.M. Jasper, and he had a cow get out. He doesn't have a brand, so there's not much chance we'd be up to that."

Hardesty pointed. "Who's this?"

"His name is Gil Simms. He works for Jasper."

"That doesn't keep you from puttin' someone else's brand on

it. You cinch-ring artists do work for any number of outfits."

"You should know."

Hardesty's face went stiff. "Don't tempt me today, you two-bit puncher. I don't like you any better than the last time I knocked you down."

Simms spoke up. "We think this is Jasper's cow. He doesn't have a brand."

"No, and he won't get one, if I have anything to do with it." Hardesty leaned on his saddle horn, and his spur clinked, as he bore down on Del. "Don't you even think about hazin' this cow back to that nester's place, much less puttin' a rope on it."

Del was conscious of having the rope in his hands. In the instant in which he was trying to frame an answer, a third rider came over the rise. Del recognized the tapaderos first, then the flat-crowned, dusty black hat and brown and yellow jacket of Lee Hilton. As he rode up, Hilton took off his riding gloves. He had his back to the slipping sun, and his bearded face lay in shadow, but Del could see his snake eyes.

Hardesty spoke again. "If you know what's good for you, you'll turn around and go back to the farm. Stay out of cattlemen's affairs."

Del met Simms's eyes, and the two of them reined their horses around. They took off at a fast walk.

Half a mile out, Del looked over his shoulder. The landscape was bare of horses, men, or cattle. "That third one was Lee Hilton," he said.

"I heard he went away."

"So did I."

A gunshot sounded from the direction of the Pyramid men. Del and Simms stopped and turned their horses.

"What do you think?" said Simms.

"I think they left something for us to see. Let's ride back to that first hill and take a look."

They rode up the rise and dismounted before they reached the top. Del led his horse and took slow steps, waiting for his level of vision to clear the crest. When it did, he saw a brown form lying still in the dry grass about two hundred yards away.

Simms appeared at his elbow. "What do you think?"

"I think it was Jasper's cow."

CHAPTER TEN

Del ate the bowl of porridge that Templeton brought him, and he did not linger over the cup of coffee. His work here was done, and he needed to be on his way. Things had ended on a cold note with Jasper, with the loss of the cow, and he had had a late supper at Templeton's. He did not feel as if he had overstayed his welcome, for he had no other place to go, but a new day was beginning.

The sun had risen on a dry, cool morning when he set out on the trail. He followed the section line south, although he did not have a destination in mind. He hadn't felt this way in quite a while—adrift, with nothing to do and nowhere to go. At least he wasn't broke. He had the pay he had collected at the Spoke, plus two dollars for his work with Templeton.

He continued south, passing by Jasper's acreage on the right. People would be working there, just as they were toiling on thousands of other little farms across the country, and on big ranches, and in towns and cities with the sounds of streetcar bells ringing, hammers rapping, and steam engines thumping. He remembered the sound of a noon whistle.

Still with no clear purpose, he arrived at Coldwater Creek, north of town. He decided to loaf for a while, so he rode upstream a ways until he came to a screen of chokecherry bushes that offered shade. He dismounted and let his horse drink.

Here, as in the patch he had seen a few days earlier, the

147

leaves were changing color. The bushes, or trees, as some of them grew to twelve feet tall, looked tired at the end of the season. All the fruit was gone, and the foliage was thinning. As Del gazed, he recalled what Templeton had said. Even though the trunks were straight and slender, they did not look so useful on closer view. The trunks turned one way or another, or branched out, and he did not see one in a hundred that was straight enough and thick enough for a stretch of five feet.

At last he saw one. He thought he should take it while he could. It might die in the winter, or someone else might cut it down. Then he asked himself where he would keep it for a year or what he would use it for until he had his own place. He imagined carrying it around, like a shepherd's staff. He laughed at his own thoughts. That was the product of not having anything to do.

He decided he would leave it there but remember where it was. He could make a gift of it, perhaps to Nuncle Wiggie, who would pass it on to Tess and let her peel it and rasp it and then use it to hoe nettles and sandburs.

A pleasant thought pushed away the emptiness he had been feeling. He could go visit Tess.

The sunshine of midmorning reflected off the whitewashed buildings as Del rode toward the Wiggins farmyard. West of the barn, in the green garden patch, a female figure in a sunbonnet and a full dress was stooping at work. Rather than ride into the yard, Del went around the barn. Tess stood up and waved, so he dismounted and tied his horse to a corral post.

She walked to the edge of the garden and met him. Her face was flushed and glowing with perspiration, but she was smiling, and her eyes were shining. She took off a pair of cotton work gloves and wiped her face with a white handkerchief. "Good morning," she said. "Did you finish your work with good neighbor Templeton?"

"I did. I worked one day for him and one day for his neighbor, in his place."

"I know of those arrangements. Lord save me from having to go thrash wheat." She dabbed at her face again.

"You look as if you've got work enough here."

"Yes, I do. I'm digging potatoes, or spuds, as Uncle calls them."

"That's hard work."

She made a casual motion with her hand. "Well, it's time to do it. I don't want to leave it all until later and then let the bad weather get in the way."

"Why don't you let me help you? I'm fresh off a day of digging a root cellar, so this should be easy."

Her deep brown eyes met his. "Are you sure?"

"As sure as my name is Jack Robinson."

"Why don't you put your horse in the shade, then, and I'll welcome the help."

Del used the spading fork. Because it had a short handle, he had less leverage than with a shovel, so the work gave him more of a strain. The soil was heavy and had some moisture, so the flat tines of the fork met with resistance. But the potatoes came up onto the loose soil, most of them intact. He creased and split some, and he impaled a few.

Tess picked them up, brushed them off with her gloved hands, and laid them in a bushel basket. After a day with Simms, who had a tendency to throw things on the ground, Del appreciated the care.

As time wore on and they were both focused on their work, Tess said, "So tell me your story. How did you come to be here, or were you born in Wyoming?"

He straightened up to give himself breath, and she stood up to listen. Her dark hair and grey bonnet and dress stood out against a vast background of rolling and broken plains.

"I wasn't born here," he said. "I was born in eastern Oregon. Timber and cattle and mining country. My father has a lumber mill, and he wanted me to be a bookkeeper. He had it all planned out. I did all right with numbers, but I didn't want to go straight into work there and be closed up for the rest of my life. So I took a job moving cattle out this way, and I stayed."

"That's a short version."

He laughed. "I'm not that old. You could guess my age, but I'll just tell you. I'm twenty-six. I've never been married or anything like it. That is to say, I don't have a second life back in Klamath Falls."

"That's in Oregon, I assume."

"Yes. It's the nearest big town. We're actually east of it."

She brushed her smudged gloves against one another. "I suppose it's only fair that I tell some of my story as well." After a pause, she said, "I'm twenty-two, but I know you wouldn't ask. I grew up on my parents' farm, as I mentioned the other day. In Indiana. My uncle needed help on his place here, so I came out to do this until I had another plan. Uncle would like me to take up a land claim here, but I prefer not to. I think he would want to manage it for me, and I would still be the woman with the hoe. Have you seen a reproduction of that painting of the man with the hoe? It strikes a chord with me."

"No, I haven't seen it, but I imagine I should." He paused. "So you're from Indiana. Mr. Templeton mentioned that he was from there, also."

"I think he and Uncle know some of the same people back there. And I suppose, to bring my story even with yours, I should say that I haven't been married, either, and I don't have a cottage back in Terre Haute."

He sensed some kind of a reluctance in her to talk about herself, and he did not want her to feel uncomfortable, so he changed the subject. "I saw something curious at the Templeton place—curious in the sense that I haven't seen it elsewhere out here. He had some rabbits in a hutch. White rabbits. I'm used to seeing chickens, but those are the only rabbits I've seen here. Domestic rabbits, that is. You see lots of cottontails."

"I didn't know that about him, but I haven't been to his place or met his wife. He's polite enough when he visits here. I think he doesn't have much company in the way of visitors, and sometimes it seems as if he's trying to get caught up on conversation. At other times, it's just 'Yum' and 'Yup.' "

Del laughed. "Yes, I can hear him. But I have to say, he treated me well."

"Oh, yes. And like I say, he's always polite here. Oh, my dear, that reminds me. It's probably getting close to noon, and I should be working on dinner. You'll stay, of course. It's the least we can do for all the labor you've done."

Wiggins had his usual composure as he sat in his place at the head of the table. He smoked from his dark, curved-stem pipe and did not seem to have broken a sweat. Del guessed that he had not made a million dollars yet that day but had thought about it. After the preliminary comments about the weather and his thanks to Del for bringing in the potatoes, which Del took to mean harvest as well as carry, Wiggins said, "So how did you fare with neighbor Templeton?"

"Well enough. I worked for him one day and worked out for him another day. He treated me well, which is to say he paid me my wages and he fed me. To be more accurate, his wife prepared the meals."

"He's all right. I don't know the missus very well, though I've been there a few times. She keeps to herself. Stork never flew over their house."

"As I was telling Tess, I was surprised to see that he had rabbits."

"Oh, yeah. They love to die in hot weather. Lotta bother to take care of."

"The day I worked for him, he sent me to a neighbor named Jasper. I worked at digging a root cellar."

"He's a good one. He does well. His daughters bring in a good share of money with all the work they do. He'll be sad to marry them off, but they're not going very fast."

"He keeps a hired man as well."

"Sure. Anyone who has a hired man for very long is makin' money."

"He did have one mishap while I was there. Some of the men from the Pyramid shot one of his cows that got out."

Wiggins shook his head in a haze of smoke. "There's always trouble with those cattlemen, and the death of that stable man in town has made folks even more nervous. There's granger people leavin'."

Del imagined farmer families packing up their churns and crating up their geese. "How much of a movement is it, that people are getting bullied around and leaving?"

"You're tellin' me about the intimidation. I didn't know it was over this way as well. Up until now, it's been to the west of us. First it was Holt Warren, and now it's another outfit."

Del perked up. "Did they attack someone else?"

Wiggins sniffed. "Nah. They just intimidate them."

"But someone is leaving?"

"What I heard. An outfit called the Palfrey, over on the other side of Holt Warren's. Of all these homestead places, they're the farthest west. The story is that they've been badgered enough, so they're packin' up everything. Leavin' a set of buildings and corrals." Wiggins puffed on his pipe. "Hope no one burns it. There's always someone who could use the wood." His overalls went up and down as he took a slow breath. "Sorry to hear the bullying is going on over here to the east. And Jasper lost a cow." Wiggins raised his eyebrows. "What are you goin' to do next?"

"I guess I'll go to town and look for work."

"No harm in that. Better than knockin' door to door and lookin' like a tramp."

Del was letting his horse drink at the town water trough when the stagecoach rolled in. A small cloud of dust rolled by as the driver brought the horses to a stop. The yellow wheels and undercarriage were spattered with mud, and the dark brown body had numerous spots where drops of muddy water had splashed up.

"Provenance," called out the driver.

The door opened, and four men stepped down. They strolled their separate ways, and they did not look as if any of them were related or traveling together. One traveler, wearing a light brown suit and derby hat and smoking a tailor-made cigarette, stopped and gave Del's horse and gear a looking-over.

The traveler said, "Are you coming into the country or leaving it?"

"Neither."

A thin man in a lightweight black suit and a flat-brimmed hat with a round crown brushed by, carrying a pasteboard suitcase strapped with a belt. "If you're smart, you'll leave," he said.

Del's eyes followed the man to identify him. It was Tom, the piano player.

"Acquaintance of yours?" asked the traveler.

"No. He was playing the piano in the saloon the other night when a fellow was shot in the street outside."

The man in the derby hat laughed. "I love the stories you characters tell. I should write them down."

"You can ask him yourself. It looks as if he's going to be traveling on your coach."

The townspeople who had gathered to see the arrival of the stagecoach drifted away as the vehicle rolled out of town with a drumming of hooves and a rattling of chains.

Del stood with his horse in the dusty street and considered what to do next. He decided to see about sleeping in the livery stable. Some men did that to save money, and he had to put his horse up anyway. In no hurry, he led Brush toward the stable. The big door was open, and a couple of horses were tied inside with their rear ends toward the door. Del walked up and peered in.

Below eye level on his right, a man was sitting in the shadows on a pile of burlap bags. Del saw him first by the orange coal of his cigarette. The man sprang up and came to a stop less than three feet from Del's nose.

A gravelly voice came out. "What'll it be?"

Del drew back. He recognized the man who had worked for the Pyramid and had then knocked on Templeton's door.

"What's the matter?" said the man.

"Sorry. I guess I expected to see someone else."

"I don't know where you been, but the crippled prince got killed."

"I think he worked the night shift."

"That's what I'll be doin', as soon as the boss gets caught up on his sleep." The man looked past Del. "You want to put your horse up?"

"Yes, I do. Regular stall, regular feed."

The man gave Del a sour look. "You're from here, aren't you? You were in the saloon the other night."

"Yes, I've been out working, and I'm back in town for a day or two."

"This is no place to make a fortune."

"I've noticed that."

"Well, you're smart. Now that I think of it, I've seen you in more than one place."

"Yes, but you haven't seen me in others, so let's just mind the business at hand. I'd like to leave my horse here, and I'll take my bag and bedroll with me."

"Why do you need your bedroll if you're gettin' a room?"

Del looked at the man straight on, noticing his bleary eyes and straw-colored stubble. Del said, "I'm not here for trouble."

With a bundle in each hand, Del made his way to the Zephyr Hotel. He had seen the business many times, but he had not been inside. His first impression was that it was in his price range. It did not have a dining room, and the lobby had only four wooden chairs. A clerk with brown hair and a grey mustache let him have a room for fifty cents. He gave Del a key and pointed the way down the hall.

Del found the room, unlocked it, and walked in. He almost bumped into the iron bedstead. The room measured about ten by twelve and had one window with the shade drawn. He left the door open to circulate the air, but he did not open the window because the afternoon sun was beating down on it. He set his bag and bedroll on the floor and stretched out on the bed. The thin cotton mattress sagged on the bedsprings in the middle.

He did not like the feeling of how he was situated, so he got up and closed the door. He raised the window a couple of inches. He heard footsteps go down the hall and was glad he had closed the door. Being on the ground floor, he did not think he would leave the window open at night.

He sat down on the wooden chair and peeked out the side of the window shade. The clapboard wall of the building next door came into view about twelve feet away. He heard footsteps going back toward the lobby.

This room would be a welcome shelter for a traveler in the winter. Any port in a storm. Some people lived out a good part of their lives in hotel rooms. He imagined a cottage in Terre Haute, with hollyhocks and a picket fence. He moved on to an image of a workingman's shack, near a railroad, where a short-faced man went home to a compatible wife and a pup on the floor. Most people weren't going to make a fortune anywhere. If a man could make an honest living, that was a good start.

He stretched out on the bed again and told himself he could tolerate the place for at least one night.

Del woke up and focused on remembering where he was. He had heard footsteps and a voice in the hall. The long shadows of evening lay on the window shade. A bit of fresh air came in through the bottom of the window.

He sat up and swung his feet around. He needed to get up and move around. He could find something to eat, maybe at the café where Jimmy the sandwich boy worked. Then he could go to the Forge and ask if anyone knew about work. He knew it was midweek with not much going on. He would have to be moderate and watch his surroundings.

Del stood gazing at the anvil on the far wall. A voice at his elbow startled him. "Hey, puncher." He turned, and although it was out of place, the voice made him expect to see a tanned, smiling face with sparkling blue eyes and framed with blond hair. In its place, he saw the powdered and rouged face of a saloon girl with puffy, dyed black hair and an arrangement of feathers that might have come from a peacock.

"Hello," he said. "You took me by surprise."

She batted her eyes. "What are you up to? Would you like to be a big boy?"

"Not tonight, thanks."

A gravelly voice interrupted. "He thinks he's too good." The man from the livery stable appeared at the saloon girl's side.

"Oh, he doesn't think that," said the girl. "I know better."

"He thinks he's smart."

"Maybe he is. He was talking to me."

"He was smart for not going with you?"

"No, for thinking about it." She smiled at Del. "Isn't that right?"

"Sure," he said.

"Don't make fun of me," said the surly man, moving to face Del.

"I'm not making fun of anyone. I'd rather you leave me alone."

Mitchell the bartender called across the bar. "Leave it be, Rand, or I'll have to throw you out."

Rand lifted his chin and fixed his stare on Del. "Meet me outside, you mugger."

Del had not heard the term used as an insult, but he was sure he was supposed to take it that way. He set his glass of beer on the bar.

The girl with the feathers put her hand on Del's arm. "You don't have to go outside. You can go to the room with me."

"If I don't go out there now, he'll be waiting when I leave."

Rand was marching toward the door, leaning forward with his fists at his sides. Del noted that he was not carrying a gun.

"Don't bother," said Mitchell. "He'll go outside and cool off. After a while, he'll come back in and pester someone else."

"I don't want him waiting for me later." Del brushed off the front of his shirt and headed for the door.

He paused at the doorway and looked both ways before stepping out. Seeing no one, he continued into the street.

Commotion at his right caused him to jump aside. Rand burst out from between two horses, milling his arms and shouting, "Here!"

He glanced a blow off Del's shoulder. Del stood back and raised his fists. Rand came forward again, knocking down Del's left fist, but Del landed a good punch with his right. He stepped back, got set, and moved forward with a one-two punch. Rand staggered back and fell on his side.

"Enough?" said Del.

Rand sat up and rubbed his jaw. "Yeah, that's enough for now."

Del walked back into the saloon, where the girl with the feathers met him.

"That was quick," she said. "You don't look like you got hurt."

"Not much."

"Did it get your blood up?"

He smiled. "Not for what you think, but I appreciate the support." He returned to the bar and found his beer.

Mitchell said, "You didn't have to go out there, but I guess it's just as well to get these things over with."

"I hope so. He could still be waiting for me later."

"I don't think he will be. He's not that tough. That's why they fired him at the Pyramid. He didn't want to do some of the dirty work, like bully around the nesters."

"He must not be that bad, then."

"Nah. He just has a chip on his shoulder."

Del was observing the meager crowd and keeping track of the girl with the feathers, even though he did not intend to do anything with her. He was wondering if he should strike up a conversation with another patron when Gil Simms walked into the saloon. He was wearing his striped cloth cap instead of his well-worn work hat, and he had on a clean set of work clothes. He searched the barroom, and his eyes landed on Del. With his chest and shoulders pulled up, he walked on over.

"Wondered if I'd find you here," he said. He gave his half-smile, which raised his cheeks and creased the upper part of his face. "Wiggins said you went to town."

"I told him I needed to look for work."

"That's what he said, and that's why they sent me."

Del did not make a connection right away. "They?"

"Yep. A group of 'em. Sometimes they do things together, two or three of 'em, and this time it's all four. There's Wiggins, Templeton, Jasper, and Bennett. Collaboratin'." Simms straightened his shoulders with a deep breath. "So I'm sort of representin' 'em all."

"I see. I don't know Bennett, but I don't think that matters at the moment."

"Not at all. He's one of them. They've got a job to do, and Wiggins mentioned you as a possibility. I put in a good word for you, said we work good together."

"That was good of you. What kind of work is it?"

"Gatherin' wood."

"Firewood?"

"No, lumber. There's a place that a little outfit is givin' up, and these fellas want to salvage the wood before someone burns the buildings down."

"Ah-ha. And what's the name of the folks who are leaving?"

Simms spoke with authority. "The Palfrey. They're just pullin' up stakes."

"And these farmers want the wood. Wiggins mentioned it to me earlier in the day, but he didn't say anything about having an interest in it or about there being any work."

Simms nodded. "They just decided this afternoon to go in on it together. What with Jasper having his cow killed, and these Palfrey people pullin' out on short order, I think they decided not to lose any time."

"I don't blame them, after what happened to Holt Warren's place."

"That's how they see it."

Del took a drink of his beer. "When do they want to start?"

"Tomorrow morning. We can meet at Wiggins's place, because it's the closest to the work. I'll be there with a wagon and the tools."

"And who-all is going to do the work?"

"Just you and me, as far as I know. I'm kind of in charge." Simms rubbed his dark stubble.

"That's all right. Will we be staying there on the job?"

"Overnight? Yeah, that's the idea. I'll plan to camp there, too. We may go back and forth as we get a wagon load of lumber, but I don't think we'll get that much each day."

"Fine with me. And just to be sure—we meet tomorrow morning at the Wiggins place. At about sunup?"

"That, or a little after. I have to drive the wagon from Jasper's." Simms smiled. "But I'm not in the biggest hurry right now. I'll have a glass of beer before I go." He nodded at the girl with the feathers. "Not bad scenery, but that's just to look at, for me."

CHAPTER ELEVEN

The sun was beginning to rise as Del stood by his horse some sixty yards out from the Wiggins farmyard. He had had a peaceful ride in the grey light before dawn, and he saw no reason to interrupt anyone else's morning until Simms arrived in the wagon. Light showed on the window shade, and he imagined Tess was fixing breakfast for her uncle. With luck, he would see her before he left for the day's work.

Quiet prevailed in the Wiggins yard. From what Del had observed, Wiggins did not keep many animals—a few chickens, a couple of growing beef calves, and a horse. Faint, muffled sounds came from the corrals. The chickens might be clucking around, and he would not hear them from this distance. He could not remember if he had seen a rooster there, and even so, not all roosters crowed at sunrise, and some crowed during the night and in the very early morning, well before dawn.

He kept an eye on the road from the east, and as objects become more visible, he saw a wagon being drawn by a pair of brown horses. It moved through the grey landscape of sagebrush and dry grass about a mile away.

Del took a couple of paces back and forth. No movement came from the farmhouse. He imagined Wiggins, clear-eyed, sitting by himself as he drank a cup of coffee and estimated the cost and the value of this enterprise.

The wagon rolled along, the dark forms becoming larger. The horses made a turn off the section line and onto the lane leading north to where he waited. The sound of horse hooves came to him, then the thump and rattle and squeak of the wagon. Simms was perched on the seat. Another sound rose on the air, independent of the combination of sounds from the horses and the wagon. Del realized that Simms was singing.

The voice died away, and the huffing, snuffling team covered the last fifty yards before coming to a stop. Simms's voice came loud over the backs of the horses.

"Been waitin' long?"

"Not very long. Enjoying the peace and quiet."

"Got here as soon as I could, but you've got to handle the horses just right."

Del saw that Simms was wearing a coat of brown sackcloth and a hat that was in good condition. The hat was dark brown, with a round, curled brim and a cylindrical crown that had a rounded top like a muffin.

Del said, "What would you think if I put my bag and bedroll in the wagon?"

"Plenty of room."

Del moved his horse close to the wagon and untied his gear. As he set his items in the wagon, he saw an assortment of items, including shovels, a pick, a digging bar, a crowbar, a sledgehammer, an ax, a hatchet, a crosscut saw, a bucket with hammers and pliers, a couple of ropes, a bedroll, a warbag, a folded canvas, and a wooden box of that kind that carried food and cooking utensils.

"Looks as if you brought plenty of equipment."

Simms smiled. "I like to be prepared. Shall we go up to the house?"

"Might as well. I'll let you go first." Del took his horse aside and swung into the saddle, glad not to have the encumbrance he had had the last few days.

He followed the wagon into the yard and dismounted. The

front door of the house opened, with lamplight in the background. He expected to see the bulky form of Wiggins in overalls, but in its place there appeared a man of middle height and narrow build, wearing a hat. As the man moved to the edge of the porch, Del recognized the light-colored hair, narrow face, and spindle nose of George Clede.

"Wait here," said Clede. "I've got some things to put in the wagon, and then we'll go." He went back into the house.

Del looked up at Simms, who held the reins in his thick hands. "I thought it was just going to be the two of us."

"So did I. But he works for Bennett. I just found out about an hour ago that he'll be goin' along. I guess he's goin' to be kind of our supervisor. That's the only change. And with three hands, we can get the work done faster. We still plan to shuttle the lumber back here as we get it ready."

Clede came out of the house carrying a duffel bag and a rucksack. "Here," he said as he stopped at the edge of the porch.

Del tied his horse and walked over to help.

Clede looked down at him with his close-set, dark eyes. "This is my personal stuff, and this is my grub. It needs to go in the wagon." His bootheels clumped as he crossed the porch and went inside.

Del put the bags in the wagon.

Clede came out, closed the door behind him, and stepped down from the porch. His hat was in almost new condition, tan, with a crease in the crown. It was of a style that a cowpuncher would use, and he wore riding boots. He said, "My horse is in the pen. You can get started, and I'll catch up with you."

Simms slapped the reins and spoke to the horses. Del led his horse to an open spot and mounted up. He did not look back.

He fell in on the left side of the wagon. A few minutes later, he heard hoofbeats, and Clede rode up to the right side of the wagon on a small-hipped, mud-colored horse.

Clede spoke to Simms. "Turn right at the road up here and go straight west. It's a few miles."

"I know the way. Jasper drew me a map."

"Just makin' sure. Don't want to lose any time."

The ranch yard that had recently been occupied by the Palfrey outfit had an unusual air about it as Del brought his horse to a stop and looked around. He saw no weeds or drifted dust or cobwebs. The windowpanes on the house were clean. The front door was closed snug. The barn door was closed, the corral gate was in place, and the water trough was three-quarters full. Based on his knowledge of the circumstances, Del felt as if he was in a village where the people had fled from an approaching army, but from appearances, a person would think that the occupants had left the place in order for the next tenants. And here he was, with two other common laborers, ready to tear it down.

Clede said, "Let's get unhitched and take a look around. I'll put my horse in here." He led the mud-colored animal to a small pen across the yard from the house, and he left it untied with the reins snugged to the saddle horn.

Del stripped his horse and put the gear in the wagon. He turned Brush into a corral that stood between the pen and the barn. Simms unhooked the wagon horses, put leather halters on them, and led them to the corral. When he turned them loose, he dropped the halters on the ground outside the gate.

Clede led the way on the tour. The open, hard-packed area of the yard ran east and west, with the pen on the north side. It was attached to the corral on the west side. The corral, in turn, was adjacent to the barn, farther to the west. The barn was not large, being twenty feet by twenty-four and eight feet high along the walls. A row of vertical posts ran down the middle of the inside. South of the barn, with room to drive a wagon between them, sat a sixteen-by-sixteen shed. Hooks and nails along the walls inside suggested that the building had been used for tack and tools.

East of the shed, across an open space where the end frames of a clothesline stood, they came to the house. It was thirty feet square with a pyramid roof, larger than a homesteader's shack but smaller than Jasper's house or the ranch house at the Spoke. Del paused at the back door before following the others inside. He turned around to see the layout he had passed through. The outhouse sat back and to the left. The toolshed was straight back, with a door facing the house and a door facing the barn. A person could walk across the breezeway into the barn, turn right, and come out through the larger door by the corral. The larger door of the barn, like the front door of the house, faced east. Del appreciated the planning and the efficiency, and he felt sympathy for the people who had invested their time and money and labor, only to be forced out. He took a deep breath. Maybe they had good judgment and knew when to quit.

Inside the house, the rooms were bare and clean. The only vestige of the prior occupancy hung on the kitchen wall—a calendar from the year before with a print of two girls in work clothes sitting on a green next to a stream and a mill. In the background, the leaves were turning yellow and orange.

All three men stood in the kitchen. Clede rubbed his chin and said, "Not sure where to start. This house is the hardest. It has a lot more to it, with more cross-nailing."

"I think we should do it last," said Simms. "We can camp in here. Take the easy stuff first, in case we get interrupted and have to leave before we're done."

"Some of the nicest lumber is in here," said Clede. "I'd like to have some of it myself. But you're right. The barn has bigger pieces. We can get a load sooner."

Simms said, "Let's unload our tools and the rest of our gear.

Put it all in here out of the weather, use this for our base. By the way, did you not bring a bedroll?"

Clede shook his head. "I plan to ride back and forth. I've got to take care of my own animals at night."

When they had all of their personal belongings, tools, food, and camping utensils stored in the kitchen, they set out for the barn with two hammers, the crowbar, the sledge, and the large iron bar.

Once inside, Simms said, "Let's start on the north end, then work our way back." He was carrying the crowbar and two hammers.

"Let's think about it," said Clede. He took out a sack of Bull Durham and began to roll a cigarette.

Del set down the sledgehammer and the big bar.

Simms had his head tipped back. "I can see a problem right away. We don't have a ladder or scaffolding or anything of that sort. I think we're going to have to build something first." He moved his head up and down. "These rafters would make good pieces for building a ladder or a couple of sawhorses. And we didn't bring any nails."

Del said, "I bet we could take apart that outhouse first, save the nails and straighten them, and have several good pieces suitable for a couple of sawhorses. Then with two or three of these planks, you'd have a low scaffold."

"Good idea," said Simms. "Bring the materials in here, and do our building in the shade."

Clede said, "What'll we use for an outhouse, then?"

Simms creased his face with a half-smile. "Same as you do in any other camp."

Tearing apart the outhouse became a two-man job, with Simms inside and Del outside. Simms tapped the boards loose, and Del pulled the nails with a claw hammer. Clede stood by and gave suggestions.

They worked well past the dinner hour at dismantling the outhouse and salvaging the lumber. They came out of it with ten two-by-fours and about twenty one-by-eights, all about six feet long, plus a great many shorter pieces on down to one and two feet. In the absence of a wheelbarrow, they carried it all to the barn so they could use any piece they wanted.

After the midday dinner, Del straightened nails while Simms cut lumber. Clede held the lumber and continued with suggestions. By late afternoon, the men had two well-braced sawhorses three feet tall.

"Them's good," said Simms. "We can use 'em on the farm after this."

Clede took a partial cigarette out of his vest pocket. He had rolled it earlier, smoked part of it, and pinched it out. Now he lit it and held it with the tips of his first two fingers and smoked at it from the side of his mouth. He said, "Too bad these people got run off. I wouldn't have had a part in it. I wouldn't take orders from those mucky-mucks. I wouldn't brand mavericks for those sons of bitches, nor run cattle onto someone else's land, nor go in and burn down their buildin's."

Simms put a pinch of tobacco in his mouth. "It's too bad, all right. You don't know what kind of hard times they had to go through to get this far, and then they have to go off and leave it."

"Hard times," said Clede. "I grew up in the Dakota Territory, and people here haven't seen anything like that. We had to use twists of grass for fire to heat the house, and we were lucky to eat jackrabbit. Others had to eat their seed potatoes and prairie dogs, but we was never that bad off." He waved at the inside of the barn with the cigarette in his two fingers. "A building like this would have been a luxury, a palace. These people had it good."

"This ain't all wheat farms." Simms spit to the side.

John D. Nesbitt

"Puh," said Clede. "You think cattlemen are kings?"

"Sometimes they have it better. What do you think, Del?"

"They don't all start out with money. Some of them build up from nothing or very little. Half the cowpunchers I know, that's their dream, to get a little place of their own and buy a few cows. Some of them never make it, but some do."

Clede spit out his words from his tight mouth. "I'm not talkin' about them. I'm talkin' about the high and mighty, like the one you worked for, that thinks he's got a right to run all over everyone else."

"I quit working for him."

"And now you're on the other side, straightenin' out bent nails."

Del drew his brows together. "I don't know what you're getting at. I worked for a living before, and I'm doing it now."

Clede squinted as he put the cigarette in the side of his mouth and smoked the last of it to his fingernails. He dropped the butt and stepped on it. "Fine with me. I didn't get to pick who I work with, but I've got to get this job done. I've got to go now, but I'll be back in the morning."

Simms and Del exchanged a glance as Clede walked away. Simms said, "We can gather up our tools and carry all these lumber scraps over to the house. I think we'll have to cook outside. They didn't leave us a stove. That'll take a while. And we need to take care of our animals. We can start taking this building apart in the morning."

Simms let Del fry the pork and the potatoes, which he did in two skillets. Simms brought a flimsy broken crate from the barn, took a seat on the camp box, hefted the hatchet, and took to reducing a slat from the crate to splinters.

"We'll have kindling for a couple of days. 'Course, we can always split some of this scrap lumber, but this thin stuff is easy. It all burns. We shouldn't be at a lack for firewood. Won't have

168

to use twists of grass. Ha-ha. Too bad Clede doesn't have a better sense of humor. He doesn't seem to have one at all. I don't know that he was cut out to be a boss, either. But I agree with him on one thing. Too bad these people got run off after all their hard work. They came here to get a new start, and from the looks of it, they did all right, and then they've got to go somewhere else and do the same thing. They'll probably make out just as well in the next place. That's the way people are. Others, they can't quite do good in one place, so they go somewhere else, thinkin' it'll be easier or they'll do better, and they end up the same."

"I've seen that, in Oregon as well as here."

"People take their poor habits with 'em, just like others take the good. At least they get a chance. Some folks don't get to. Like this fella whose place we drove past in the mornin'. Holt Warren. I didn't know him. But it's too bad. You always think you'll see good weather and a new season come around again. That's me. I work hard and look forward to the next thing. I want to have my own place. Just gotta work and stick with it."

Sunlight flowed through the end of the barn as the boards came down. Simms knocked the boards loose, Del pulled the nails and saved them, and Clede stacked the lumber. Some of the nails were harder than others to pull, so Del went back and forth between using the claw hammer and the crowbar. Clede watched, and each time a clean board was available, he set it on the stack.

Simms had been singing a sentimental song about a miller's daughter whose hair turned to grey as she waited by the old millstream for her sweetheart who never returned. When he finished the song, he spoke in a loud voice from inside the building.

"We're goin' to wish we had a ladder for the rafters and the roof, but we can get the walls first. All these posts are good, but we can't get to them until we take the top off."

Clede was standing in the sunlight, away from the building. The sky was clear, and the day was already warming up. He wiped his brow with his cuff and said, "Maybe we should do the roof now, before it gets any warmer. I know it can get hot working on a roof."

"I'm just gettin' the swing of it here." Simms stepped up to the opening in the wall and pointed upward with the hammer handle. "That's gonna be slow work. You've got battens, tar paper, and roof boards."

"That tar paper gets hot as hell. That's why you want to do it now."

Del had known people who liked to change what other people were doing or planning, and he thought he might be seeing that trait in Clede. Also, he had a good idea of who would be working on the roof and who wouldn't.

Simms looked at the inside of the roof. "I don't like to change what I'm doing already, but I can see one good thing. As soon as we get two rafters down, we can build a ladder."

Del was crouched on the roof, prying off battens with the crowbar, when he saw two riders approaching from the southwest. He paused for a moment until he recognized them as Jim Price and Ed Westfall. They were riding side by side in no great hurry, Price on a dark horse and Westfall on a light one. Del went back to work, steadying the crowbar as the roof vibrated. Simms, standing inside on a sawhorse, was pounding to loosen the ends of the lower roof boards.

Price and Westfall rode around to the eave on the northwest corner of the building, where Del was prying up the end of a batten. Price was wearing a blue neckerchief and his wrist cuffs with blue snap buttons. He called out in his cheerful voice,

"The people you meet in places you never expected."

Del said, "I should say so. What brings you boys out this way?"

"The boss sent us over to the Cornish Buttes." Price pointed to the west. "Mostly Pyramid cattle over there, but a few Spoke. We heard the hammerin', so we thought we'd come over. There's usually girls and fried chicken at a barn raisin'. But it looks like you're doin' the opposite."

"The folks who had this place pulled out."

"We heard that. The boss told us to come by here, see if any rustlers were hangin' out."

"He's still promoting that idea, is he?"

"Seems to believe it."

"How about Macmillan? How's he doing?"

"The same. The boss sends him out on his own, but he'll hire someone to pair up with him on roundup."

The hammering had stopped. Del did not see Clede, but Simms had come out through the open end in the wall and walked around the corner of the building. He raised a thick hand and said, "Howdy."

"Same to you," said Price. "I see you've got some work under way. Who's doin' it, if you don't mind my question?"

"Not at all. My boss, J.M. Jasper, went in with three other men to salvage the lumber here."

Price leaned on his saddle horn. "I see. Just curious."

"Sure. And if you don't mind my askin', what was the name of the place you said you went to? I was inside, and I didn't hear it well enough."

"The Cornish Buttes?"

"That was it. I thought you said Cornish. They use it for the trim on the inside of houses."

Price said, "Cornish are like Welshmen. Coal miners and hard-rock miners, though I don't know of any mining out there.

I think they use the name for hash, too, but I'm not sure." He lifted his chin toward Westfall. "Shall we be on our way, Ed?"

Westfall pushed his spectacles onto the bridge of his nose. "Mise well."

The two punchers rode away, in no more of a hurry than when they came.

Simms said, "Some of your old pards, I take it."

"They ride for the Spoke, where I used to work."

"They don't seem so bad."

Del cast a glance at the two riders sauntering along as their horses swished their tails. "They do their work. It appears that their boss sent them over here to check on us."

Del was peeling up tar paper in the hot afternoon when the sight of a second pair of riders put a knot in his stomach. Rich Hardesty and Al Fisher approached from the south, the direction of the Pyramid. Del walked to the north end of the roof and leaned over the open end of the building.

"More company," he said.

Simms had been singing "Bringing in the Sheaves" and now stopped. "Be right there," he said.

Although it was laborious to climb back onto the roof, Del decided to go down. He did not think Hardesty and Fisher would pay as sociable a visit as the Spoke riders did. Once on the ground, he brushed himself off and tucked in his shirt. Simms met him.

"These two are from the Pyramid," Del said. "Foreman and right-hand man. The ones we met the other day."

Clede made himself scarce again as Del and Simms walked around to stand on the shady side of the building, in front of the main door.

Hardesty and Fisher rode into the yard in front of the house and continued to the barn. They had their usual facial expressions, a scowl and a smirk, as they brought their horses to a stop. Hardesty was riding his shiny sorrel, and Fisher was riding a hammer-headed buckskin. Hardesty gave the site a looking-over until he settled his wide, brown, but not expressive eyes on the two workers.

"What's going on?" he asked.

Simms answered in a relaxed tone, "Doin' a little work."

"Hard to tell what kind. Looks like a mess to me."

"Ah, that's just tar paper we've been takin' off the roof."

"What for?" The curtness of the question carried the tone of a threat.

Simms raised his shoulders as he took in a breath. "Well, we're reclaiming some lumber here, on behalf of a group of men who went in together to make kind of an association."

"Who are they?"

"You might know 'em. Their names are Wiggins, Templeton, Jasper, and Bennett. I work for J.M. Jasper."

"I know that. Who's in charge?"

Simms pushed up his lower lip, and his chin shortened. "Well, I hired this man here, and I kind of put things together, but there's a fellow inside who reports to the association. You might say he's the actual supervisor here."

Hardesty's dull eyes went from Simms to Del and back to Simms. "An association," he said. "Sounds like a big one."

"Just some men who put their resources together."

Hardesty let the silence hang in the air.

Simms shifted his eyes to Fisher. "So what are you boys up to?"

Fisher gave his insolent blank stare and said, "Just me and my chicken."

Simms frowned. "I don't follow you."

Fisher pointed his thumb at Del. "Ask him."

"He has an imaginary pet chicken he likes to tell stories about."

"Oh." Simms looked at the ground.

Hardesty's horse shifted position, and the foreman's voice came out loud. "We're on the lookout for rustlers. We want to make sure they don't use this place as a hideout."

Simms raised his head and put on a faint smile. "I assure you there won't be any rustlers staying here."

"That's why places like this get burned down."

"Well, now, there's no hurry. Let us get the good lumber out of here first. No need to let it go to waste."

"You're a long ways from the farm."

Simms's smile was gone, but he was hanging onto his composure. "Like I told you, we're just doing our work. The men we work for sent us over here to do this job, and we're not causing any trouble to anyone."

Del expected Hardesty to tell them to go back to the farm, but he said, "I already told you what we think." The foreman gave a brisk head motion to his right-hand man, and the two of them pulled their horses around and took off at a gallop.

Del watched the dust drift away. "I didn't think about it while they were here, but I'm glad Hilton wasn't with them. I wonder where he is."

Simms said, "I wish they would leave us alone."

Del shook his head. "Don't count on it."

CHAPTER TWELVE

A cold wind was blowing from the northwest with a grey sky overhead. Tar paper was flapping against the corral, and some pieces had blown into the yard. To cook breakfast and make the morning coffee, Simms and Del had to move the site of the fire to the east side of the house. Even then, the wind came around, so they set up the outhouse door, which they had not yet taken apart because of all the clinched nails, against the wooden camp box for a windbreak. By the time the potatoes were fried and the coffee was boiled, all the scrap lumber under three feet long had gone into the fire.

Simms said, "We'll have plenty of scrap as we go along. I expect several of these roof boards not to come off in one piece. We've got some long splintered ones already. Once we get the roof off, this whole job should go faster." His face creased as he blew steam off his coffee. "I would have been happy to keep takin' off all the wall boards, even on the shed, too, to get as much as we can for a load or two. But some of the best lumber is in the studs and rafters, and those posts in the middle are worth the work. None of this wood is very old."

Del held the warm coffee cup with both hands. "I think it would have been better to take the easy stuff first. Get what we could while we could. I didn't like Hardesty's tone yesterday. Not that I ever do."

"The other fellas weren't so bad. The ones you used to work with."

"I'm not worried about them."

"Well, here's Clede. He'll wonder why it took us so long to get through breakfast. He should have been here to appreciate it."

Del had finished stripping all the tar paper and had come down from the cold wind on the roof when a saddled horse walked into the yard. Del's abdomen tensed as he recognized the long-legged pale horse and the plain saddle with slick forks, a low cantle, and rounded skirts. With Macmillan missing, the animal had a ghostlike quality.

One of the horses in the corral whinnied, and the pale horse answered.

Clede opened the large door of the barn and stood in the doorway, cupping his cigarette as he took a drag. "What's that?"

"It's a horse from the Spoke outfit, and the saddle belongs to the fellow I rode with. Name of Macmillan. The horse is from his string."

"Musta throwed him."

Del frowned. "Not him. And not that horse."

"I think you should put it in the corral, or tie it up outside. Someone'll come lookin' for it."

Del took slow steps into the yard and let the horse walk up to him. He laid hold of the trailing reins and patted the horse's neck. He did not see any blood or scuff marks on the saddle.

He led the horse to the lee of the building, where Simms had joined Clede. "This doesn't look good," he said. "Macmillan wouldn't have let a horse run away on him, and this one never gave him any trouble that I saw. It's a top horse."

Clede said again, "Someone'll come lookin' for it."

Del looked the horse over. It couldn't tell him a thing. He said, "I think we should go look for him."

Clede took another drag. "We can't waste the time. We've

lost time already. This is the third day on the job."

Del fixed his eyes on Clede. "You just don't leave a man out there."

"It's none of our affair. Let these cattlemen solve their own problems, take care of their own."

"I used to ride with him. He'd do the same for me."

Clede looked past Del as he spoke. "We came here to get work done. We don't have time to go on a wild goose chase."

"Well, I'm going. If no one wants to go with me, that's fine."

Simms spoke up. "I don't have a saddle horse here." He turned to Clede. "If I could borrow yours, or at least your saddle . . ."

Clede looked Simms up and down, as if he was estimating his weight. "I'm supposed to be in charge of gettin' this lumber claimed. I can't let everyone go off lookin' for people who get lost."

Del said, "I don't think he's lost. I think he's in trouble. Or worse. I'm going to look for him, and you can dock my pay if you want."

Clede dropped the snipe of his cigarette and ground it with his heel. He said, "I'll keep track of it."

Del took the pale horse to the corral, put it in with the two wagon horses, and took Brush out. As he curried and combed and saddled his horse, he went back and forth with himself about whether he should take Macmillan's mount. At last he decided to go by himself, as it would allow him to cover more ground with much less trouble, and he did not know if he would find anything.

The cold wind blew as the clouds moved overhead. A huge bank of clouds in the northwest, with shades of white and grey and charcoal, seemed to have an unlimited supply. The air smelled like moisture, but no drops fell.

177

Del had not seen the pale horse before it walked into the yard, but he thought it came from the south, as he had not seen it in any of the other directions where he happened to look, so he went that way first. Once he was out on the open plains, he had a sense of how hard it would be to find a person who was not standing up. The land had rolls and dips and rises, as well as buttes, clay bluffs, breaks, and gullies.

He recalled a story he had heard from a man who had his own little ranch and was thrown by a headstrong horse a couple of miles from home. He had lain the whole night on the prairie as his wife drove back and forth in a wagon, a mile away, with a lantern in her hand. His ribs were cracked, and he had the wind in his face. When he tried to holler, it felt like a whimper, and the wind carried his voice away. Del wondered if Macmillan had spent the night watching for searchers or if he was beyond seeing the night sky.

Del pushed his horse. He saw cattle with the Spoke brand, the Pyramid brand, and three or four other brands he was familiar with. He did not make an effort to keep track of the cattle, whose brands he read by habit.

He saw antelope at a distance, always a distance when the wind was blowing. He saw a couple of lone bucks, a doe and a fawn, and a group of three. At a water hole, a group that was sheltered from the wind rose up and trotted away. Out of habit, he counted them. Eight.

Small birds tacked and floated on the wind. A grasshopper hit him on the cheek. From high above came the scree of a hawk. He saw no magpies, no buzzards, though he thought to keep a lookout for them.

He worked his way back and forth across the country north of Coldwater Creek. North of him lay the homesteader claims, two of them abandoned now. West and south would be the Pyramid. South of the creek, in the area he knew best, sat the

Spoke headquarters, where Macmillan had saddled the long-legged pale horse and where Lawna, at this minute, might be looking out the window and wondering when the rain would fall.

Del did not want to get caught in a rainstorm. At this time of the year, the rain began light and steady, became colder and heavier, and lasted for a day or more—not like the summer rains, which blew in and blew out in a few hours.

All this time, he searched in the grass and sagebrush. He saw forms on the ground that turned out to be anthills, gopher mounds, prairie dog hills, and one badger den. He came upon a tattered flour sack, half-covered with caked dirt and debris. He stared down at a single grey leather glove, its palm slick and dark with wear and the first finger torn open and frayed at the end. It was a work glove, such as a freight hauler or a road grader would use—or for all he knew, a hard-rock miner. Although the palm still had a faint shine, the glove had been flattened by rain and time.

With no sun in sight, Del lost track of time, but he thought the noon hour had passed. He had not given himself an amount of time after which he would call it quits. He would either search until he found something or give up when he thought he had looked long enough.

He found something. It began as a long, low form in the sagebrush and became more visible as he rode closer. He saw worn, wrinkled boots with spurs the size of two-bit pieces, then denim trousers, a brown cloth vest, a grey shirt, and a bearded face. Closer, Del saw where the man's hair thinned on top and gave way to a bald spot in back. A dust-colored hat lay on the shortgrass a yard away. With his heartbeat rising to his head, Del fought himself to stay calm.

A dark spot in the back of Macmillan's vest had a hole in it.

Del paused a moment to take off his hat and say, "I'm sorry,

Mac." He sniffled, rubbed his eyes, and put on his hat. He looked around to make note of landmarks, and then he set off at a lope in the direction of the Palfrey.

Clede was holding an eight-foot, one-by-eight when he heard the news and Del's insistence that they go for the body. He threw the board on the ground and said, "If it ain't one damn thing, it's another. Now we're saddled with this."

Simms said, "How should we do it?"

Del kept his attention on Simms. "I think we should go in the wagon. We'll have to take him to town, but I think it will be too late in the day to go all the way. Wiggins is closer. It would be a little farther overall, but we could put up for the night."

Simms had a calm demeanor. "How far is the body from here?"

"About two miles south of where we are now. Maybe halfway between here and the creek, where it curves around to the north."

Simms said, "We're a little north of Wiggins right now. We could pick up the body and not come back here. I don't want to leave our tools and belongings here, so I think we should pack everything up." He turned to Clede. "Unless you want to stay here and get more done."

Clede shook his head. "Oh, no. I'm not staying here by myself, and I've got to go home tonight anyway." He huffed a breath out through his nose. "This is a hell of a mess."

Del took a look around, and he had to agree. Tar paper lay flat on the ground in some places and flapping in others, as well as clinging to the corral rails. A small pile of splintered lumber sat near the stack of salvaged lumber, several yards away from the barn. A few boards were gone from the roof, and he could see the top of the skeletal end wall. The way the wind was blowing, it would bring in a few tumbleweeds and move some dirt around, and before long the place would look like a ghost town.

Simms walked over and picked up the leather halters where he had left them on the ground two days earlier. "I can get started hitching the horses if you two want to put the tools in the wagon. It won't take me a minute to roll up my bed. Del, you can put your stuff in the wagon any time. The camp box, too. We had cold grub for lunch. There's some in the box if you want it."

As soon as they had the tools in the wagon, Clede said, "We don't need three men to go out and pick up a body. I can head on home and let the bosses know what's going on." In another minute, he was leading his horse from the pen and turning out his stirrup.

With Macmillan's horse tied to the back of the wagon, Del rode alongside and directed the way to the spot where he had found Macmillan. Nothing had changed. Del and Simms cleared a space in the bed of the wagon, laid the body in, and covered it with a canvas.

Simms put a pinch of tobacco in his mouth. "I'm sorry to see this. I know he was a pal of yours."

"Thanks. We rode together. I thought I'd see him again before long."

Simms turned the wagon east and headed in the direction of the Wiggins homestead. Before long, he was singing a dirge-like song about an orphan boy who went through a wicket gate to visit his mother's grave and to carve her name upon a tree.

A flash of light color caught Del's attention. Off to the south, two riders were headed in the direction of the wagon. Price and Westfall, both riding sorrel horses, were moving at a brisker pace than they were the day before.

They caught up with the wagon and fell in alongside. Price spoke across to Del. "We've been out looking for Macmillan.

He didn't come in yesterday, so the boss sent us out this morning. We've been all over but didn't find anything. That looks like his horse."

"It is," Del answered. "It wandered into our work this morning, so I took it upon myself to go out and look for him. When I found him, I went back for help."

Price tipped his head up. From the saddle he could see into the wagon box with no obstruction. "Is that him there?"

"Yes, it is. Someone shot him in the back."

Price let out a long *wheww* sound and said, "By God, there *is* someone out here sneaking around. Do you think he came up on someone who was doing something? You don't think he was up to anything, do you?"

"I don't think he was doing anything himself. And if he came up on someone, whoever it was had the skill to shoot him in the back."

Price's face had a clouded expression. "It doesn't make sense. I don't think the boss is going to like it one bit."

"I suppose you should take this horse with you. It belongs to the ranch. The saddle is his, of course."

"Sure," said Price. "I wasn't even thinking of that. Where are you taking him?"

"To town. But I don't think we'll make it any farther than Wiggins tonight."

"That's good to know. Someone's bound to ask."

Simms stopped the wagon, and Del dismounted to untie the horse with Macmillan's saddle. He left the lead rope in the wagon and handed the reins to Price.

"I'm sorry to be the one to tell you this, Jim. He was our friend."

"He sure was," said Price. "This is a dirty thing to happen."

As the two riders took off through the sagebrush, Del asked Simms to hold up for a minute. Hanging onto the reins of his own horse, he walked around the wagon until he could reach his duffel bag. He opened and felt around until he found his six-gun, holster, and belt. He took out the rolled-up object and closed the bag.

Simms said, "Good idea," then sat around straight and put the wagon into motion again.

The wind continued to blow, but rain did not come. What few cattle Del saw were grazing in low spots, out of the wind. No other riders or travelers appeared. Simms drove the wagon and kept to himself, and Del was left to his own thoughts. With the sun behind the cloud cover, and the irregular series of events during the day, he had an uncertain sense of time, but he guessed it was past five in the evening when the white buildings of Wiggins's homestead came into view under the grey sky.

As the wagon creaked into the yard, Clede and Wiggins came out of the house and stood on the porch. Wiggins had his hands in his overall pockets, and he was moving his mouth as if he was cleaning his teeth with his tongue. The bib of his overalls went up and down as he stared at the wagon.

"Looks like you made it all right," he said. "Hell of a thing to happen. George says you're having a hard time making progress on the job. But I don't think we should let this stop us. You can take this into town in the morning, and unless it rains, you can be back on the job in the afternoon. We just need to make sure the associates know what's going on." Wiggins turned to Clede, took another labored breath, and said, "George, you can go to Templeton's and then to Bennett's and tell each of them, and then go on back to your own place as you need. We'll meet here in the morning."

Wiggins shifted and spoke to Simms. "You can back the wagon into my barn. It can stay there overnight. Meanwhile, you go to Jasper's and let him know. You come back here in the morning, too, of course."

He turned to Del. "I've got you figured to spend the night in the barn. Not that I expect anything to happen, but it seems right that someone should keep it company."

"I can do that. We've got food in the box, so I'll be no trouble to anyone."

Clede made an abrupt *hmmh* sound. His mouth was set firm as he rubbed the underside of his chin. He said, "I didn't know I was going to have to go to two other places."

Wiggins shrugged. "It's not that far. And you can go back to your own place."

"I thought I would let it go for one night, stay here, and get an early start in the morning."

Wiggins gave a light lift of the eyebrows. "There's nothin' says you can't get out of here by seven in the morning."

"I didn't know we were going to do things this way."

With his hands still in his pockets, Wiggins straightened his shoulders and gave a bland smile. "So that's our plan. Meet here in the morning, and take this to town. You can get back to work on the project, and we'll let the proper authorities find out what's going on with this other business."

Simms said, "I'll need a saddle to ride one of the horses over to Jasper's."

"Oh, sure. I've got one. George can show you where I keep it."

Del was sitting in the barn in the light of a kerosene lamp when a light knock sounded on the door.

"Come in," he said. He stood up from the grain box he had been sitting on.

The door opened, and Tess walked in. She was wearing a dark wool overcoat and carrying a cup of coffee with steam rising from the surface. Her hair was loose, and she had a red ribbon tying a tress on one side.

"I brought you this," she said. "I didn't know how late you wanted to stay up or if this would keep you from sleeping. You don't have to drink it if you don't want to."

He took it from her. "Thank you. I want to get some sleep if I can, but I don't think this will keep me from it. It's been a tiring day."

Her eyes met his. "I'm sorry for what happened to your friend."

"Thank you. It's a difficult thing to think about. He wasn't much older than I was, maybe thirty, and now everything is over for him."

"It seems very unfair," she said. "People console one another for the loss when someone dies, but the people living have not lost anywhere as much as the person who has died. And yet, as they say, life is for the living."

"Oh, yes. I'm sure my friend here would want us to go on and live life the best we can. But it's still not fair, especially in this case."

Her face grew firm. "And then we have George Clede, and to some extent my uncle, who see this as an inconvenience to them. George spent a while this afternoon expostulating on how this has been a great interruption to the work, and how it happened because you insisted on leaving the job. I'm sorry. I know that telling these stories just makes things worse, but he seemed so . . . insensitive. Self-centered."

Del did not want to seem too eager to malign Clede, so he said, "I don't find him very cooperative."

"And then there's my uncle and his associates, as he calls them—his business partners in this little venture as in others. They stay within their safe bounds and seem to think that these things happen only to other people. Don't you think?"

"Something like that. A neighboring homesteader gets pushed

185

around and goaded into a fight. The next people over are intimidated to the point of packing up and leaving. A man in town is killed. And they proceed as if it was a hailstorm or a hoof-and-mouth disease that was someone else's bad luck." Del motioned with his head toward the wagon that sat at the edge of the lamplight. "Now this."

He took a drink of his coffee.

She said, "I didn't mean to come out here and complain about all these others. But once I started—"

"I know what you mean. You don't always get to talk to people who see things somewhat the way you do."

She smiled. "Isn't that right?"

He laughed. "It might be a matter of the company a person keeps. Of course, if you work for a living, as we both do, sometimes you don't have much of a choice of company."

She raised her eyebrows but did not look straight at him. "Yet it doesn't seem as if you're stuck where you are."

"Oh, I could leave. I know that. One of the reasons I've stayed around has been to see if there was anything I know, or anything I could do, that would help right some of the wrongs that have gone on. But it seems as if things have just gotten worse, and people who know too much don't fare well."

"Is that what happened to your friend?"

"I don't know, but that's my hunch. He was friends with a fellow who knew too much, the man who was killed in town, and he was curious to ask me what I knew." Del held up his hand. "Because I didn't know anything for certain, I didn't say anything. I thought we might share knowledge later, but of course that didn't happen." He glanced at the wagon and then at the door. "I feel funny talking about these things here."

"We can go outside," she said. "It's not bad, just a little windy. But that way you won't have the feeling that you're talking about somebody or that someone's listening at the door, which of course they're not."

"I wouldn't mind going outside. Let me find a jacket."

Clouds were moving overhead and not in solid banks, as stars became visible and then disappeared. Del and Tess walked along the southern edge of the garden.

"I thought it was going to rain," he said, "but there isn't as much moisture in the air as there was earlier."

"We could use some rain for the garden, but not if it's followed by a frost."

"I think it might be early for that. Today's just the thirteenth. But you can't count it out." He took in a breath and felt his lungs fill. "What were we talking about? Oh, yes. Reasons why I don't leave. I think I covered the first one enough."

"Are there very many?"

"Only one other to speak of. But I don't want to talk out of turn."

"You have the floor."

"What I mean is, I don't want to say something if I didn't think our . . . conversation was at that point."

She glanced at him sideways in the faint moonlight. "It's just the two of us."

'Well, I'll be blunt, then. The other reason I've stayed around is to see if there is any interest between you and me."

"By that I gather that you might have some interest. I don't think you have to ask me if you do."

He gave a short, nervous laugh. "Of course I don't. That is, I don't have to ask you about that part."

"But you are asking about the other part."

"I suppose. You see, that was what I didn't want to rush into if there wasn't much of a basis to it."

"I wouldn't rule it out," she said, "but I think two people need to know each other before they become very interested, so it's not all on the outside. You know, just a surface attraction."

"Oh, I agree. But I'm afraid I'm not very good at going through lists, such as what a person likes and doesn't like."

"Yes, and that's all rather preliminary, unless there was something big that would get in the way."

"Such as?"

"Oh, whether a woman should be able to vote or to have property in her name."

"Those things are covered by law, aren't they? At least in Wyoming, women are allowed to do both of those things."

"Yes, but some men are opposed to things that the law favors or allows."

"I see. Well, I'm not opposed to those things."

"They are just examples. There could also be things that one person might not tolerate, such as tobacco, alcohol, or gambling. A person should know to ask about them. But there are other things that only the individual knows—things that the other person should know about, rather than find out when it's too late."

"I think I know what you mean. Personal history, or personal background."

"Something like that."

He stopped at the corner of the garden, where the grass and the sagebrush stretched away in the dim light. "Something that the other person should know. Well, for me, there might be one thing. It seems to have a big place in my early life, though I couldn't tell you of a specific influence it has had."

"Go ahead."

He looked out into the night and saw the old story that was always there. "It starts when I was six years old. For reasons I've never known, my mother left me with my father. They fought, and I was shuttled back and forth, and then she left me with him. He was busy with his business, so he left me to live with my aunt and my uncle and my cousins. I lived with them, and everything seemed normal, and then one day a woman came by. It was a rainy day, and she was under an umbrella, and she had brown hair. I didn't recognize her. But my cousins did, and they all started running and shouting, 'Auntie Peg! Auntie Peg!' That was my mother's name, Peg, so I realized who this woman was. She had changed the color of her hair. When she came around to me, she said she was going away but she would come back to see me. I didn't feel very much one way or the other about that, because she hardly ever came to see me as it was. So she went away, and I didn't think very much about her, until one rainy day in November when I was eight, my aunt and uncle told me my mother had died in Seattle."

"And that's it?"

"I suppose so. That seems to be the part that matters. It's how I always remember it. The last time I saw my mother, I didn't recognize her. As far as what kind of a fact that is about me, one thing that has set me apart from other kids, growing up, was that I didn't have a mother."

Tess sniffed. "That's a sad thing to hear, the whole story. But you seem to have come through it well enough."

"Maybe I have, but I don't know if, deep down, it has made me yearn for a woman's attention or if it has made me distrustful of women, as if I expect them always to leave me. You can tell I've thought about it. I'm not good at analyzing myself, but it seems to me I've seen traces of those tendencies."

She said, "I don't find it frightening or discouraging."

"Thank you. Maybe I should add that I don't think I'm in search of a mother. I've thought about that as well and looked into myself. To the contrary, it seems as if I've grown a hard shell that allows me to do without one."

"You don't seem so hard-shelled to me."

"It's different with a girl." He laughed as before. "It had better be."

"Oh, yes," she said. "You know, the wind is not that cold."

"No, it isn't."

"We could walk again."

As they had reached the west corner of the garden, they
turned and began to walk north along the edge where the
pumpkin vines sprawled out onto the prairie grass. Del waited
for Tess to speak.

"I suppose it's my turn, like before." She paused. "My story
comes from a little later in life. As I've mentioned a couple of
times, I grew up on my parents' farm. My father raised corn
and beans, and my mother had a large number of laying hens.
They had all the other things, too, such as milk cows, calves,
sheep, and hogs, as well as other crops that my father dabbled
in, such as millet, sorghum, and soybeans. Anyway, I worked at
all of these things, and like other youngsters on the farm, I
became restless when I became, you know, older. Sixteen and
seventeen. And so I got into trouble with a young man who
came through on a harvesting crew." Tess took a couple of steps
before she continued her story. "My family made the decision
for me. That is, my parents. I did not have a choice. They sent
me to a home for unwed mothers, and I stayed there until my
term was up and my baby was given away. Then I went back
home, to work under the watchful eyes of my parents. No one
in our town or on the neighboring farms said anything, but I
could tell they knew. I was damaged goods. People left me alone.
Then the chance came for me to come out here, for a new start,
of sorts. But I'm not much more than a servant here, and as I
mentioned before, I don't want to take up land and have
someone else manage it for me." She let out a sigh. "It's not a
very long story, but it's a hard one to tell, and I don't have it
very well practiced."

"It's a touching story all the same. I'm sorry you didn't have more to say about such a big choice."

"It was the way things were, and my parents and I were never able to be on very good terms after that. There was always that thing between us, which for them was what I did, and which for me was what they took away."

"It has to have an effect."

"Indeed it did. But as I listened to your story and heard myself telling mine, something occurred to me that I had not thought of before."

"What is that?"

"I have not been in search of a son." After a second, she said, "I'm sorry. What I mean is, I haven't been looking for someone to fulfill that role."

"That's good."

"As for having children, that's different. It's in my vision of the future."

"That's good, too. I don't have a clear vision of my own future, but I have always assumed kids were there."

"All of that in its time," she said. "For right now we're just a boy and a girl, or a man and a woman, two people who meet and wonder if they're suitable for one another."

The clouds overhead had parted for the moment, and a few stars were visible at the same time. Del said, "That's a good place to start. I haven't heard or seen anything that is, as you say, discouraging. It seems to me that we are two people who are not perfect and could be compatible in understanding that about one another."

She slowed in her step. "I think it's one thing to be not perfect, because everyone is that way, in spite of appearances, but some of us are flawed."

"I know what you mean. There have been many times, especially when I have heard others talk about their mothers,

191

when I have felt incomplete, as if I had a part missing, or a hole in me, and it was something I didn't choose."

"Maybe we are more similar than I realized."

He said, "I don't see any large obstacles or impossible differences. If I come out of this other obligation all right, and I mean this job your uncle has us on, I'd like to continue as we are."

"I would like that," she said.

His eyes closed as they moved toward one another under the stars as the wind blew on the edge of the prairie.

CHAPTER THIRTEEN

Clede arrived as the sun was breaking over the eastern hills. Simms had ridden in half an hour earlier and had the horses hitched and the wagon ready in front of the house. Del stood by his saddled horse. As Clede's horse trotted into the yard, the colors of his clothing caught the morning light. He was wearing a close-fitting tubular sweater, yellow with red horizontal stripes, and a large, red, lightweight bandana knotted on the left side. He rode his mud-colored horse right up to the wagon and stopped.

Simms said, "Good lookin' sweater, guy."

Del kept himself from laughing. He thought Simms's use of the word "guy" went along with the modern style of Clede's garment.

Clede said, in his sullen voice, "It's called a pullover. I had to wear it because my coat was in the wagon, and I didn't know how cold it would be on the ride over."

"Air's pretty still right now, but the wind can always pick up later in the day."

Wiggins appeared on the porch with a coffee cup in his hand. "Looks like you boys are ready to go. Any word from the others?"

Simms spoke up in his calm voice. "Jasper's all for it, just like you. He says go ahead and get what we can. I told him I thought the work would go faster now."

"Good. And the others?"

Clede gave a grudging glance. "Same."

"Well, fine. Don't waste any time in town."

Simms slapped the reins and spoke to the horses. The wagon lurched into motion, and the group moved out. Del did not look back. Tess had kept herself scarce all morning. Clede looked over his shoulder once, and Del almost felt sorry for him until Clede settled into place and said, "Let's remember who's in charge today."

Townspeople gathered as the wagon rolled into town and came to a stop. From the muttered comments, Del gathered that the news had made it to town ahead of them. Clede swung down from his horse and made his way in full color to the barbershop. The day being Saturday, customers and conversationalists had already gathered, and a couple of them had come out onto the sidewalk to watch. Clede marched past them and into the shop.

He came out a minute later, took his reins from Simms, and said, "Pull around to the alley."

Del followed. Down a gauntlet of small stables, woodsheds, and hollyhocks gone to seed, the wagon stopped at the back door of a business on the left. A larger door next to it rolled aside, and the barber stepped out, a dark-haired man in a white shirt, black bow tie, and grey apron. He pulled out what looked like a high worktable mounted on wheels. A folded sheet lay at the far end.

The men made the transfer in a matter of minutes. Simms shook out the canvas and spread it in the back of the wagon. "A little sun and air," he said.

The sun had climbed to midmorning when the wagon pulled around into the main street. With a man on horseback on each side, Simms brought the horses to a stop in front of the general store. He said, "We should think about anything we need while we're here."

Clede, sitting on his horse on the street side of the wagon, said, "Don't know what it would be."

Simms scratched his chin. "It might be early in the day for some people, but I wouldn't be opposed to a glass of beer. It *is* Saturday, and we won't be able to come in later on."

"There's plenty of time for that some other day," said Clede. "Unless you need coffee or beans—"

"I could go for some licorice." Simms rose halfway from the seat.

"Make it quick."

Simms draped the reins on the dashboard and let himself down backward onto the ground. His short, round form made a slow descent, but he took off at a quick walk, his arms swinging at his sides.

Del dismounted and stood with his horse between the wagon and the sidewalk. A voice at his right made him turn.

Lawna and her mother stood in the shade of an awning. Lawna was wearing a sky-blue dress, and her mother was wearing a pale yellow dress. They both wore white straw hats held on by wide, white ribbons.

Del moved closer and, nodding to Diana, took off his hat. To both of them, he said, "I didn't expect to see you here."

Lawna spoke. "Bill sent us in. He's all worked up. He says with all the trouble on the range, he can't be sure how safe it is at the ranch. He says it could get worse during roundup."

Diana, in her proper voice, said, "We were very sorry to hear about what happened to Oswald Macmillan. I know you worked with him, and so you were friends. I'm sure it was difficult for you to be the one to find him."

"Thank you. It was a hard time, to be sure. His horse wandered into a place where we were working, and I had my fears from the beginning."

Lawna spoke again, her tone a little more brash. "Bill says it's rustlers. He says now that they've struck his men, they could do anything."

Del brushed Diana with his glance, and she did not seem ruffled. To Lawna he said, "Do you believe that?"

"I don't know what to believe," she said. "Rich says the same thing."

Del tossed away his sense of caution. "Sure he does. And yet one of his men pulled the trigger on Holt Warren."

Diana gasped, and Lawna's blue eyes widened. Then her eyes narrowed, and she said, "No one ever told us that. All we heard was that he died. Bill didn't want to talk about it."

Del tamped down the indignation he felt rising. "That's the danger of coming to town. You can hear it from anyone." With his hat still in his hand, he directed his attention to Diana. "I'm sorry to have been so blunt about it, but there's two sides to a story."

Diana's eyes showed a woman busy in thought. "We were all friends long ago. People pass on, but—this is not a good thing to hear."

"I'm sorry. Perhaps it wasn't my business to be the one to let you know."

Her eyes seemed still to be searching, but they settled on Del. "Not at all. That is, you don't have to apologize at all for telling the truth. Sometimes it seems as if we've lived too long at Happy Valley Ranch."

Del took in both women again. "I don't need to say any more. I know you're both capable of judging for yourselves." He lowered his voice and looked around. "People do pass on, and they take knowledge with them. Sometimes that's the reason they die. But some of the knowledge lives on. If for some reason you don't see me again, there's a woman in this town named Maude who was a friend of Holt Warren. She knows things that he knew." His eyes met Lawna's and then Diana's. "I'm trusting you with this, trusting that you won't give her name to the wrong person or people. She's not a woman from your walk of life, but she believes in the truth."

Lawna said, "I'm not afraid."

In a quieter voice, her mother said, "Perhaps the time has come. We will see."

Simms was finishing his licorice stick about a mile out of town when Clede called for a halt. He took off his colorful sweater and neckerchief, folded them, and stowed them in his canvas bag. He was still wearing a plain, collarless work shirt with three buttons, with a light vest over that. After making sure of his tobacco and papers, he gave Del a light glance and said, "Who were those women you were talking to?"

"Wife and stepdaughter of Bill Overlin, owner of the Spoke. I did work for both of them as well as for the boss, so they know me. They were telling me they were sorry about what happened to Macmillan."

"Seemed like a pretty cozy conversation."

"It was between us. And I don't work there anymore."

"Yeah, but you're still part of that world, aren't you? Talk to your uppity friends. Just a little better than the rest of us."

"Think what you want. You've seen how well I get along with the Pyramid boys."

"Hah. I heard the foreman brags about knockin' you down."

"I don't know who you heard that from."

Simms looked at his shoes.

Clede said, "Don't matter."

"No, it doesn't," said Del. "He did knock me down. He punched me when I wasn't looking. Right after he punched Jim Price, the fellow with the blue bandana who came by. Price said it was because the foreman was frustrated about not doing well with women."

Clede hardened his close-set eyes. "You've got a story for everything."

"How many have you heard?"

"One is too many. We're wastin' time." Clede stuck his foot in the stirrup and hauled himself up into the saddle. As his horse was about to take off, he pulled it back. "That was his girl you were talkin' to, wasn't it?"

"Yes, it was."

"No wonder he punched you." Clede loosened his reins, spurred his horse, and burst out ahead.

Del had a couple of ideas for getting in the last word, at least with Simms, but he let it be. He smiled, Simms shrugged, and they continued on their way.

The group had not gone another mile when a rider overtook them from the direction of town. Del did not recognize the man. He looked like a townsman, as he was wearing a sand-colored shirt and matching trousers, plus a brown cloth vest. He wore a plain hat with a round brim and a short crown, and instead of riding boots, he wore shoes. But he rode with competence, and he brought his horse to a smooth stop.

Simms and Clede and Del all turned to face him as they held their animals still.

The man looked them over and asked, "Which of you is the one who found the body yesterday?"

"That would be me," said Del.

Clede interrupted. "Who are you?"

"My name's Bird. I work at the feed and seed. They sent me because no one else could go."

"Who sent you?"

"The deputy. He just came to town, and he wants to talk to the man who found the body. That's all. He said it shouldn't take long."

"Why didn't he come?"

"He's busy."

Del said, "I can go. I shouldn't be gone for much more than an hour. At the very least, I can catch up before you make it to the Palfrey."

Clede said, "I don't like it. It's just another interruption."

"It's the law who wants to talk to me."

Clede reined his horse around and said to Simms, "Let's go."

Del took off at a lope with the man from town. In less than twenty minutes, they slowed their horses at the edge of town.

Bird waved his hand. "The deputy said he'd be in the café."

"Thanks. I'll find him."

Del tied up in front of the café and went in. The noon hour had passed, and the deputy sat by himself at a table. He had a badge pinned to his leather vest, and his hat hung on a peg in back of him. He rose and held out his hand as Del approached his table.

"How do you do? I'm Deputy Todd with the Laramie County Sheriff. Thanks for coming. Have a seat."

Del took off his hat and sat down. Something about the deputy seemed familiar until Del realized that he bore a resemblance to the foreman of the Pyramid, with his brown eyes, muddy complexion, and light mustache. Deputy Todd was older, though, in his middle to late thirties.

The deputy picked up a pencil and poised it at the edge of a sheet of paper. "So are you the man who found the deceased man named Oswald Macmillan?"

"Yes, I am."

"And your name?"

"Del Rowland."

The deputy made a check mark next to Del's name, which he already had written on the page. He put on a thoughtful expression and said, "When did you find the body?"

"Yesterday, around the middle of the day, maybe a little after noon."

"September thirteenth."

"Yes, sir."

"And where was it, as nearly as you can tell me?"

"I would say it was about two miles north of Coldwater Creek, about five miles west of here."

"Straight west?"

"No, north as well. The creek curves north at that point, and the body was two miles north of the creek."

"I see." The deputy wrote down some notes. "And what position was the body in?"

"It was lying facedown, stretched out, with the head northwest of the feet."

The deputy wrote as he asked his next question. "Was there anything that would indicate to you when the time of death might have been?"

"Well, two fellas who work with him said he didn't come in the night before."

"That's what they say. We'll stick to what you know. I'll take care of this other on its own. Their names are Price and Woodhall, correct?"

"Westfall."

"Oh, yes. That's what I have here." The deputy peered at Del. "So, to put it more clearly, was there anything you observed that would give you an idea of the time of death?"

"Two things. The horse he rode, wearing his saddle, came into a place where we were working about two miles north of there. That was in the middle of the morning, between nine and ten. I went out to look for him, and I rode back and forth until I found him, as I said, around the middle of a cloudy day, and I kind of lost track of time."

The deputy continued to write as he spoke. "I understand.

And what was the other thing?"

"The body was stiff."

"When you found it?"

"No, a couple of hours later, when we picked it up. I didn't touch it when I found it."

"Just as well. Unless you think there's any chance the person is still alive."

"I didn't think so. I could see the dried bloodstain on his back."

The deputy looked up and trained his eyes on Del. "I understand you recently left the ranch where you had been working with Macmillan. Did you have any hard feelings against him, or did he have any against you?"

"Not at all. We were friends. We rode together."

"When was the last time you saw him alive?"

The picture came to Del's mind. "Right here in town. By the water trough."

"When?"

"It was last Sunday, the eighth. In the middle of the afternoon."

"And what did you talk about?"

Del paused to think. "People we knew. A friend of his had been shot here in town the night before. Macmillan and I were in the saloon together at the time."

"Malcolm Bain. That's what brought me to town today. As soon as I got here, I found out about Macmillan."

Del did not have a comment.

The deputy continued. "Do you know of anyone who might have had reason to do harm to Oswald Macmillan?"

"Nothing that I know of first hand, and nothing I can think of from anything he said."

"Or to do harm to Malcolm Bain?"

"Again, nothing that I know. You'd have to ask his friends."

John D. Nesbitt

The deputy pushed out his lips. "Back to Macmillan. Did either of you owe the other one money?"

"No. Never did."

"Did either of you have anything on the other, in the sense that one of you knew about something that the other one did?"

"No, not at all."

"Were you sweet on the same girl?"

Del smiled. "No, we didn't cross paths there."

"Did he have anything to do with some else's girl?"

"Not that I know of. If he did, I would be surprised."

"Why?"

"There aren't that many girls around."

"Or wife?"

"Again, I have no idea, but I doubt it. I don't know how I would know, even if it happened. And I don't understand why you're asking me."

The deputy shrugged. "Those are the main reasons men kill each other. One of 'em is money or property. One of 'em is women. And one of 'em is that one man has something on the other."

Del shook his head. "I don't know of anything."

"Well, if you hear of anything, don't be afraid to let me know."

"You said you didn't want me to report what other people said. Just what I know."

"That's correct." The deputy smiled. "Thank you for your help."

"Thank you for your work. I hope you find whoever did this."

"So do I."

Del walked out into the daylight and found his horse. Brush was dozing with a hind foot lifted. After the short rest, he should be good for the return trip. Del led him to the water trough and let him drink, then tightened the cinch a notch and swung aboard.

As he turned around in the street, he decided to go around through the alley in back of the barbershop. Riding in the opposite direction from before, he passed the sliding door, closed now. He touched his hat and said to himself, "Goodbye, friend."

Down the alley a ways on his right, past a clump of hollyhock stalks with a scattering of dried purple and pink blossoms on the ground, he glanced up and saw a familiar person sitting on the back porch of an unidentified business. Maude was seated in a wooden chair, wearing a tan-and-blue housedress and holding a coffee cup in her lap.

He stopped his horse and swung down, crossed in front, and spoke across a distance of fifteen feet. "Do you mind?"

She studied him for a couple of seconds. "No, come on in."

He approached, leading his horse, and he stopped at the foot of the wooden steps.

"What is it?" she asked.

"I saw you here, and I thought there was something I should say to you."

"I'm sorry to hear about your friend."

"Thank you." He lowered his voice. "As you can imagine, it has been troubling."

"There's nothing good about any of this." Her hazel eyes went to his horse and came back to him. "What is it?"

Still in a lowered tone, he said, "I took the liberty of giving your name to someone." He held up his hand. "Two women." Lowering his voice even further, he said, "A woman Holt Warren would have died for, and her daughter. I think they are beginning to see things in a better light."

"And you told them I might know something?"

"Yes, I did. I trusted that they wanted to know the truth, and I believed they were skeptical enough to know to be very careful."

"I wish you hadn't. People who know too much end up dead."

"I realize that."

She frowned. "Why didn't you just tell them what you heard from me?"

"A couple of reasons, I think. For one, I didn't know if they were ready to hear it. They had just heard from me how Holt Warren died, and they seemed to be putting things together. The second reason is that the closer a person is to the source, the more believable it is, or so it seems to me. I told them that you believed in the truth, and I told them I trusted them not to give your name to the wrong person."

"I wish you hadn't, but it's too late now."

"I didn't know if it would be too late in some other way. If something were to happen to me, they wouldn't know that someone could tell them something."

Maude's eyes had a weary expression. "I don't know. They're from a different world, you know."

"In some ways, they are closer to you than I am, or than they are to me."

"By being women. Well, it's not always the same. Some women will never forgive a soiled dove for what their husbands take it upon themselves to do."

"My sense was that they were on their way to wanting to know the truth."

"Even at that, some people have a hard time giving up their illusions. That goes for men, too." She drank from her cup. "Thank you for what you said about me believing in the truth."

"Well, thank you for not being too put out with me. I suppose I should be going. I need to get back to work. We were on our way when I was summoned to talk to the deputy."

"I heard he was in town."

"I didn't give him your name, by the way. But he may have questions for you. He said he came to town to look into what happened to Malcolm Bain. Then this other thing dropped in his lap."

"We'll see how far he looks."

"Very good. I'm on my way."

"Be careful."

Del caught up with the wagon at about a mile from the Palfrey buildings. He fell into place along the right side.

Simms said, "Everything go all right?"

"Normal, I'd say. The deputy asked all the questions you would expect."

"What was his name?"

"Todd. I'm surprised I remembered it."

"Don't know him."

"He came a long way."

Although the sun was shining, the Palfrey layout looked as desolate as it did the day before. Del thought it would not last long enough to become a genuine ghost town, although it had already had one ghost horse come through.

Simms pulled the wagon to a stop in front of the house. "Shall we unload all the stuff?" he asked.

"That can wait," said Clede. "We need to get some work done today. Let's put the horses away and pick up where we left off."

Del unsaddled Brush and put the saddle, blanket, pad, and bridle in the wagon. As a second thought, he took off his spurs and hung them on his saddle horn. They had created an annoyance when he was working on the roof and when he crouched for some of the work on the ground. Simms unhitched the wagon horses and put them into the corral with Del's. As usual, Clede left his mud-colored horse saddled as he put it into the smaller pen.

Simms said to Del, "We ate on the way. You could grab a

quick bite if you wanted."

"I'm not that hungry. I can wait."

Del turned and found Clede blocking the way.

"I want to have a word with you first." Clede's narrow face had a red tinge, and his jaw muscles moved. "You need to remember who's in charge here. I don't like the way you went off and did what you wanted yesterday. Those other two would have found him soon enough. As it is, you caused us to lose more than a day's work, not to mention get mixed up in that business."

Del did not answer. He recalled Clede's earlier taunt about Hardesty knocking him down, and he thought Clede might want to try to do the same.

Clede started over. "So that's the way it's gonna be. You do what I say." He raised his hand as if he was going to peck Del on the chest, but Del put his arm in the way.

"Keep your hands off of me."

"Well, aren't you brave?" Clede's dark, close-set eyes held steady. "Let me tell you something." He raised both hands in a quick motion and pushed at Del's chest.

As Del stumbled back, Clede stepped forward and pushed him again. Del lost his footing and fell on the hard-packed ground.

Keeping an eye on Clede, Del turned, brought his knees under him, and pushed himself to his feet. "I told you to keep your hands off of me."

Clede's tight mouth opened and closed as he said, "So you did."

"Well, let's finish it, then." Del stepped forward and glanced a blow off Clede's upraised arm. He took half a step back, moved in, and landed a left punch onto the side of Clede's face. The tan hat tumbled away. Del came around with a right and planted his fist on the side of Clede's mouth. Clede fell back and hit the ground.

Del stood close but not towering over. "We should be even now," he said. "I don't think there's a need to carry it any further."

Clede stood up, retrieved his hat, and put it on. The side of his mouth was redder than the rest of his face, and his small, pointed teeth became visible as he said, "It doesn't change anything. I'm still the boss on this job."

Del could feel the surge in his arms and chest, but he was settling down. "I never said you weren't."

CHAPTER FOURTEEN

The fair weather prevailed as the afternoon work got under way. Blue sky showed through the spaces where end boards had been lifted off the east side of the roof. Daylight poured in from the north end, where the workmen had taken off the first boards. The skeletal wall made for easy passing in and out of that end of the building, and it also let in the cool breeze. Light clouds moved overhead. From time to time, a heavier cloud lingered, reducing the sunlight and lowering the temperature.

The men had taken down two rafters and had them laid out on the barn floor to make a ladder. Del was crouched at one end, holding the two-by-fours on edge so Simms and Clede could nail on the steps, which were split pieces of one-by-eight roof boards. Del was glad he had taken off his spurs, but the six-gun at his side kept getting in the way, as he was not used to wearing it when he did manual labor.

Clede held the steps in place as Simms did the nailing. Simms was singing a song about a tramp who died of starvation and was found in the street by a night watchman. The nailing was slow, as Simms hit the nails with a light *rat-a-tat* to keep from bending them again, and he took his time positioning himself for each set of three nails. Meanwhile, he took irregular heavy breaths and sang the song about the tramp in the street.

"Good God," said Clede. "Can't you save that singing for some other time, when you're workin' by yourself?"

Simms stopped hammering and singing. "I suppose I could. I

didn't know it bothered anybody."

They moved on from the second step to the third one. They put the board in place, and the *rat-a-tat* picked up.

A change in the sunlight at the end of the building caused Del to look up. He felt a jolt in the pit of his stomach as he registered three men on horseback coming to a stop and turning their horses to face the building. He recognized all three in an instant—Fisher, Hardesty, and Hilton. They dismounted without making any noise that Del could hear, and Fisher took the reins of the other two horses.

When the hammering came to a rest, Hardesty's voice sounded. "Come out here!"

All three workers rose to their feet. Clede signaled to Del with his hand and said, "You stay here. There'll be less trouble that way." He pushed Simms's elbow. "Go out and see what they want."

Simms set the hammer on the floor, hitched up his trousers, and walked toward the end wall with his hands hanging away from his sides. He turned sideways and squeezed between two studs, then walked a few steps more to face the visitors.

His calm voice carried. "What do you fellas need today?"

Hardesty said, "We came to burn this place down."

Simms raised his hand to waist level and turned it palm up. "Oh, we're just gettin' started. Let us get some of this lumber out of here."

"Look," said Hardesty. "I already warned you."

Simms said, "We've got just as much right as anyone else to come here and salvage. All we want—"

Hilton cut in, and his voice gave Del a chill. "Who are you to tell us who has the right?"

"Just another citizen. Like you."

"Tell your friends to come out."

"They might be busy. Why don't you leave us alone?"

A gunshot blasted. Simms hunched up, staggered a step to his right, and fell in a heap.

Del stood rooted, not knowing what to do. Clede broke and ran.

Del pulled his gun. He was sure that Simms was past any help. Fisher was getting the horses settled down as Hilton and Hardesty advanced toward the building with their guns drawn.

Clede ran back to the main door, flung it open, and bolted out. Del ran after him, trying to keep his thoughts in order. Clede had a saddled horse ready in the pen. Del's horse was loose and unsaddled, in the corral closer to the gunmen. He stopped at the door.

Clede ran past the front of the corral, fumbled with the gate on the pen, and pulled his horse around and around in a circle until he could stop it. He stuck a boot in the stirrup, climbed on, and bent over as the mud-colored horse charged out through the gate and thundered away.

Two gunshots went after him.

Del brought his thoughts back to himself. Three on three had gone to three on one in a minute. He had six shots.

Hardesty was coming through the open end of the building. Del figured Hilton had fired the shots outside, from the other end of the corral. Del recalled that Hilton had cartridges on his gun belt. He would be reloading.

Del ran out through the small door of the barn, across the breezeway, and into the toolshed. As soon as he was inside and trying to catch his breath, he realized he was trapped, or would be, if Hardesty came to one door and Hilton to the other.

Del was breathing hard, and he felt empty, but he had to do something. He searched his memory fast. He was sure he had closed the door to the barn behind him. Hardesty was not moving fast. Del had to do what they would not expect.

He rushed out through the door he had just come through,

and he cut to the left. At the end of the breezeway, he turned right and ran in soft steps along the west wall of the barn. Ten feet from the corner, he paused. He was in full sunlight, and the warmth reflected off the wood. The breeze was not as strong here as it was on the north, where Fisher was holding the horses. This was a safe place, but it would be that way for only a few minutes.

He walked along the wall, taking one slow step at a time and keeping a watch over his shoulder. He covered the last two feet a few inches at a time, then jerked back when he saw the hind end of a horse. He did not want a horse to see him and whinny. He took off his hat and drew his gun.

He edged up to the corner again. Fisher had his back turned, but his brown hat with the rounded crown was unmistakable.

Del's heart was pounding again. He had to do it. He couldn't think about how he was going to go up against all of them. He had to take this one and see if he could lay hands on a horse.

He put on his hat, drew back the hammer of his pistol, and stepped into the open. A sorrel horse jerked its head up and around. Fisher pulled on the reins as he turned. Surprise showed on his face as Del aimed his pistol with both hands and fired.

The horses exploded, squealing and grunting and kicking, as Fisher collapsed. The horses stampeded, and Del was left on his own. He could not go back the way he came.

He crouched and ran, past the open end of the barn and past the corral. He crouched behind the northeast corner of the corral, not far from the empty pen. He did not think the two gunmen had seen him, but they would have heard the shot for sure. He heard voices, and he placed them between the barn and the shed. The horses in the corral were looking in that direction as well.

Del did not think he had a chance at shooting it out in the

open, and he did not like the idea of being cornered like a rat. He thought he might be able to ride his horse bareback, clutching the mane, but he did not know how he would get it out of the corral. He pictured himself making a run for it on foot across the open country, but he despaired at the thought of being run to the ground by two men bent on killing him. His first burst of fear had taken a great deal of energy out of him. He felt some of it coming back, but he did not know how long he could run. Even if he did, Hardesty knew Del's horse, would find his saddle, and would ride him down.

Del wondered if he could get at least one of them by staying close. His heart jumped when he saw Hardesty emerge from the open end of the barn with his gun drawn. The foreman took a few slow steps and paused, looking at the ground where Del guessed Fisher was lying. Hardesty raised his head and scanned the country to the north, where the horses had run. Then Hardesty did something that took Del a minute to understand. After holstering his gun, he walked to the pile of splintered lumber, knelt, and began picking up pieces and cradling them in his right arm. He was going to start a fire.

Del thought it out. Each building they burned was a place he couldn't run to and hide. If they had a good fire going, they could burn a body or two. He would have to wait to see where they began.

Hardesty stood up and disappeared into the barn with an armload of splintered lumber. A few seconds later, the large door on the east side of the barn closed. Del placed both men inside the barn, and he figured they were going to start the fire in the corner by the two doors.

Again he had the urge to run for it, but he knew they would come after him as soon as they had the fire going. He had to get at least one of them. He thought he could outrun Hardesty by himself if it came to that, unless Hardesty had Del's horse. Still, he had to try to do away with at least one of them, and Hilton would be the better choice.

He ran along the east side of the corral and pen, stopped, and dashed across the open area to the house. He pulled up behind the house and peeked around. Both doors to the barn were closed.

He ran around the house, past the spot where the outhouse had stood, and on to the corner of the toolshed. He heard voices from inside the barn. He moved along the east wall of the shed and slipped in through the door that faced the house. He crossed to the other door and listened.

The door opened inward, and he had not closed it all the way when he went out a little while earlier. He stood by the crack.

Hardesty's voice made him flinch. "That's goin' pretty good. Let's open these two doors now, and the wind'll help. I'll go get some more of this broken stuff."

Del sank back. He heard the door across the way creak open. He drew his pistol as he heard someone take a couple of steps, pause, and take four more. Del's heartbeat went up as he expected Hilton to appear. A hand made a small bump on the door and pushed it open. Hardesty stepped inside in no hurry, with his hand on the butt of his pistol. As he turned to survey the interior of the shed, his eyes went wide, and he clawed at his pistol. Del fired.

He took a second to make sure it was Hardesty lying on the floor. The broad face, muddy complexion, and sparse mustache left no doubt. Del glanced at the man's boots and saw that he had taken off his noisy, large-roweled spurs.

Del's heart was pounding in his throat as he ran out the other door and raced for the house. Once inside, he leaned his shoulder against the door. He tried to make sense of what had just happened. He was sure he had heard Hardesty's voice, but it had come from inside the barn. It didn't make sense for Hilton to offer to go get the second armload of wood anyway. Del wondered if it was a ruse for Hardesty to peek into the shed. He didn't think so. If it was, Hilton would have been waiting at the other door. Del imagined that he had either heard wrong or missed something else that was said. Then it occurred to him that it could have been something as simple as Hardesty opening the smaller door of the barn and deciding, in a casual and confident moment, to take a look inside the shed before he went for more firewood.

Whatever the case, Del had it down to one, but not the one he would have wanted to deal with last. He was sure Hilton could keep a calmer nerve, shoot better, and maybe even run faster. The one way Del might have an edge would be on horseback.

His saddle was in the wagon right outside, but trying to use it was out of the question. That would be as good a way as any to catch a bullet in the back. But getting away on bareback was still a possibility, and it might not occur to Hilton to look for a saddle and catch up one of the wagon horses.

Hilton would not waste much time when he found Hardesty. He might be on the way to the house right now. Del stepped to the edge of the back window and inched toward the pane for a peek. He snapped back when he saw dark-bearded Hilton, in his flat-crowned black hat and brown and yellow jacket, with his pistol drawn, heading for the door that Del had just passed through.

Del did not see a lock on the door, only a keyhole. He ran through the small house, opened the front door, and listened. When he heard the back door open, he ran for the corral.

Flames were visible through the barn door, smoke was seeping out between the boards on the roof, and the horses were milling. Del did not dare to leave the gate open until he was sure of his own horse. But he wouldn't be able to open it once he was on Brush's back.

He thought fast. He reached under his gun belt, unbuckled the belt that held his trousers, and pulled it off. He would put it around Brush's neck and hold him that way until they were out of the corral. He had no time to lose.

Thicker smoke was coming from the barn, and the horses would not stand still. They kept each other moving around. Del tried not to keep his back to the house as he stepped one way and another in an attempt to get his arm around his horse's neck.

A gunshot ripped the air, and one of the wagon horses reared up with a scream of agony. A second shot dropped it. Del did not know if Hilton was clearing the way for a shot at him or was going to shoot all the horses first to keep Del from getting away.

Another shot crashed, and the second wagon horse let out a long, rumbling grunt and stood immobilized in shock. Blood trickled out on the side where Del was standing. He caught a glimpse of Hilton straddling as he leaned on the gate and aimed.

Del gave up on trying to catch his horse and moved to the hind end of the wounded animal. He drew his pistol and found Hilton, who was drawing down for another shot at the horse, which was standing in a daze. Hilton fired, and the horse lurched.

Del figured he had four shots while Hilton had two. He held his pistol with both hands and fired three shots between the rails of the gate. Hilton fired one shot that split the air over the back of the horse. Del fired again, but Hilton was falling by then. His pistol tumbled off the inside of the gate and fell in the dirt and dry manure. A second later, the wounded horse fell with a rush and a thump that stirred a small cloud from the ground.

★ ★ ★ ★ ★

The fire had broken through the roof of the barn and was burning cleaner, with less smoke, than a few minutes earlier. Before
long, it would engulf the whole building, and given the way the
breeze was blowing, the fire might jump to the shed.

Del returned his attention to saddling his horse. His hands
were still shaking as he pulled the cinch and put the spoke of
the buckle into the hole. He had almost no energy. He could
stand, but lifting the saddle onto the back of the horse had
taken a concentration of effort.

He sucked in a breath and took a drink of water. With his
horse tied to the wagon wheel, he rummaged in his duffel bag
and found his box of cartridges. His fingers fumbled, and he
concentrated again to push the shells into the cylinder.

His eyes wanted to close, and he made them stay open. He
had to put his spurs on. His hand seemed a little steadier as he
lifted the spurs from his saddle horn. Kneeling was work, and it
pushed the breath out of him, but he got his spurs buckled on.
He pushed himself up and laid his hand on the saddle horn to
be sure of his balance.

He could hear the flames as well as see them. If he had the
strength, he could go into the end of the building that had not
burned yet and retrieve the tools, but it was too much to think
of. If the fire jumped to the shed, the building would burn
down on Hardesty's body, but the prospect of trying to drag all
that dead weight into the open was beyond his consideration.

Del did not know if the three gunmen had come with the
primary intention of killing the three workers. If they had, they
might have gone about it in a more methodical way and would
have cut off the route of escape. Perhaps they had come to burn
the place down, as Hardesty said, and things took a turn when
Hilton cut in. Del thought back to the moment when Hilton
told Simms to tell his friends to come out, and Del remembered

the chilling sense that he might be facing execution. Then everything broke loose.

Maybe Hardesty did not come to kill first, but he went along with it right away. And he had taken his spurs off. As for Fisher, he had stood by, untroubled, while Simms lay dead in the grass a few yards away and the other two went after Del. To hell with all of them. It was kill or be killed, and it could have had a much different outcome.

Del untied the halter rope from the wagon wheel and exchanged the halter for the bridle. He stowed the halter in his duffel bag. He would have to come back for his belongings later. It was too much work to tie it all on and then swing his leg up and over. He had to ride, and just getting onto his horse loomed as a challenge.

He led the horse out into the open and tried to lift his foot to put it in the stirrup. He could not lift it high enough, and it would not stay steady. Hanging onto the reins and saddle horn with his right hand, he pulled his knee up with his left hand and held it. The tip of his boot went into the stirrup. He gave a hop and pushed it in far enough, then gave another hop as he pulled himself up with both hands on the saddle horn. He gathered his reins and caught the other stirrup, and he was ready to go.

Energy had seeped back into him once already, and he hoped it would again. But he felt washed out. He hadn't eaten anything since morning, in Wiggins's barn. He needed to go there now. He was on a big circle, from Wiggins to town to the Palfrey and back to Wiggins. That was the closest. Maybe Clede would find help, but he would have to go farther to do it.

Del reasoned a little further. Clede would have to go to town. He might even have gone there first. That was where Del had to go. Men had died, and he had a hand in it. He had to account for himself. Town was farther, but not by that much. He had to go there. He wasn't going to make a circle today. Del blinked his eyes once, twice. He reined his horse thirty degrees to the right and kept going at the horse's steady pace.

Del did not look back as he rode across the rangeland. As soon as he felt a little more strength in his arms and legs, he would put the horse into a lope. But for right now he had to keep it to a walk.

He still felt empty, and he remembered that he hadn't eaten. He also realized that there had been food in the wagon and he could have found something to eat fast if he had had the presence of mind. Now he would have to wait until he made it to town.

Out of the landscape on his right, a man came riding. Del told himself it could not be Hardesty or Hilton. It did not look like Bird, the messenger from earlier in the day. He did not think it was Deputy Todd.

The horse was loping. Across the distance, it was silent, as through a pair of binoculars or in a motion picture. Del recognized the shape now—the hat, the build of the man, the way he clung to the zebra dun that he mounted with a mounting block.

Overlin was not trying to cut him off. He was riding ahead, turning around to meet him. The yellow and black features of the zebra dun, as well as the boss's blue suit, caught the afternoon sunlight.

Del summoned his energy as he rode the last few yards and came to a stop facing Overlin. He kept his hands steadied on the saddle horn.

Overlin spoke in a friendly tone, but Del knew the serpent beneath the flower. "And what are you up to today, my young friend?"

Del cleared his throat. "I've been working at the Palfrey, salvaging lumber." He saw that Overlin was not wearing his usual riding gloves.

"I heard that. It doesn't look like you're doing any work right now."

"I need to send a telegram, but I need to stop at my boss's place. Maybe you know him. His name is Wiggins."

"I've heard of him. I hope everything's all right, having to take off to send a telegram."

"Oh, yes." Del did not know what he was going to say next. The words came out. "It's just something about my inheritance."

"Is that right? Where is it that you're from?"

"Oregon."

"John Day? That's the one place I know."

"Klamath Falls is closer."

"I've heard of it. No trouble over at the Palfrey?"

Del's pulse jumped, but he shook his head. "Oh, no. Just got to look out for snakes when you turn over a board."

"That's everywhere. The reason I ask is that I thought I saw some smoke from over in that direction."

Del kept himself from turning around. "Huh. Not while I was there. Could be, though. I've had my back to it for the last little while."

Overlin's eyes narrowed. "You don't look good."

"I think I ate some bad grub. They gave me some mutton stew."

"That's what you get from these shit-pot outfits." Overlin lifted his reins. "But I'd better let you go. You've got things to do. I just thought I'd see who was out here riding where I've got my cattle."

"Good enough, sir, and good afternoon to you." Del touched his hat.

"The same to you."

Del rode forward and passed by within six feet of Overlin and the zebra dun. The boss of the Spoke smiled. His face was flushed and damp with perspiration, but it was a perfect wall for not showing any feeling or intention.

A few steps farther, Del turned his horse to the left. As he did, he saw that Overlin was doing the same thing, except he was drawing a .45 and pointing it. Del kicked his horse.

The shot ripped past, sending a concussion of air against the side of Del's face. The zebra dun started bucking, and Overlin dropped the gun. The horse turned as it was bucking, and Overlin pitched off and landed with a thump. His hat bounced on the ground as the horse took off with a flapping of stirrups and a pounding of hooves.

Del stopped his horse and turned it.

Overlin scrambled to his feet, with the sunlight shining on the bare spot on his head with the little tuft of hair visible.

Del did not think of whether to run or stay. His only thought was that he needed to get to the gun first. He spurred his horse forward, pulled to a stop, and swung down. He drew his gun, with no more definite thought than taking this man prisoner. As he turned from his horse, some ten feet from the man in the blue suit, he saw Overlin's hand coming out from inside the jacket, then the glint of sunlight on a snub-nosed revolver. As the barrel came around and the hammer clicked, Del fired his own pistol.

A red dot appeared on the white shirt above the notch where the blue vest was buttoned together. The owner of the Spoke took a step to the right, dropped his gambler's gun, and fell to the earth.

CHAPTER FIFTEEN

Deputy Todd sat across the table from Del with a full sheet of notes in pencil. "You came out of it better than your friend George Clede led us to expect. I had to finish with a couple of other witnesses, and that was the next thing I was going to do, see if I could get some men to go out there. I'll still have to do it, but I have a more definite idea of what we'll find." He shook his head. "I've been in this line of work for ten years, and I'm still surprised at what men will resort to."

Del pushed his empty plate away from him. "As long as they think they can get away with it."

The deputy smiled. "That's the criminal mind. They always think they're a little smarter and won't get caught."

"I was thinking of the ones who did more brazen things, as I've heard it put, because they knew others had gotten away with it. But it looks as if this case has a combination of the two."

The deputy's head wagged in a small motion. "One thing we learn is that human nature doesn't change. Men commit the same crimes and have the same motives one generation after another, one century after another."

Del was not sure that the deputy understood his comment, but he let it go. He could tell that the deputy wanted to be the one at the table who knew the most. He said, "Have you gotten a better idea of who might have killed Malcolm Bain?"

The deputy waved his hand. "It's all circumstantial. I've

talked to a couple of his friends—a Mr. Drayton and a Mrs. Underhill. You might know her as Maude."

"Oh, yes."

"From what I understand, Malcolm Bain had information he had learned from Holt Warren, some of it leading to the possible guilt of Mr. Overlin in the death of the first Mrs. Overlin." The deputy raised his eyebrows. "It even leads to the possibility that he had something to do with the death of Paul Gresham. I understand that you have heard all this, so I don't need to go into detail."

"That's true."

"So, to make things brief, men who died were men who knew things, though it's not clear how much. Or to put it another way, if there wasn't something to be known, these men wouldn't have died. That may well have included your friend Oswald Macmillan."

"He was skeptical of what Overlin was up to with all of his talk about rustlers, and he did seem to want to know more."

"So this goes back to my earlier point about the reasons men kill each other, or pay someone else to do it. Number three. One man has something on another. And we ask why. Number two. A man has or had designs on another woman. And what else does he have to gain? Number one. Property and money. So it makes a neat case. We've got the perfect criminal. But the problem is that all we have is hearsay and circumstance."

"So there's no perfect truth in this case."

"Unfortunately, no. I even talked to Mrs. Overlin, and that was before you brought your news, and she seemed inclined to believe some of the theory about her husband's earlier motives and the death of Holt Warren, but again, no proof."

"Well, I know one thing for sure. More than one man tried to kill me today. I may not know the perfect reason, but I know they had one."

"Yes, and they're not going to be able to do it again. Here's a way to look at it. There's a fellow I know out by Bear Mountain, had trouble with something getting into his pastures and killing his calves. He thought it was a wolf. So he studied the almanac, stayed up a couple of nights when the moon was full, and killed himself a big wolf. The trouble with his livestock quieted down, but he couldn't be sure the wolf he killed was the animal that killed his stock. On the other hand, he was sure the wolf killed something in the past, and it didn't kill any more."

Del said, "So if you don't have perfect truth, you don't get perfect justice. But you get some. Like the case of Tom Horn, if it ends the way some people hope."

"I don't have an opinion about that," said the deputy. He brightened again. "You've had a rough day. I won't ask you to go out there with me. I'm sure I can get some men."

"You'll want to have a couple of new wagon horses as well."

"Oh, yes. What I was going to say is, even if I don't need you right now, I'll ask you to stay around for a day or two until I'm sure I have all the information straight."

"Can I go out to the country to see my boss?"

"That should be all right. Just don't leave the area."

"Very good." Del rose from his chair and nodded to the boy, Jimmy, who had come to take his plate. Del took a couple of steps and found himself steady on his feet. He thought he had enough in him for one more visit today.

Del and Tess walked along the edge of the garden in the moonlight. Off to the right, dark pumpkin plants rose a couple of feet high, and their large, round leaves caught the silvery light. To the left, the grassland stretched away with clumps of light-colored sagebrush dotting the view.

Tess said, "So even if almost everyone is certain of who did these things and why, there's no proof."

"That's the way it is. But even if this person didn't do the worst things he is accused of, which I think he might have, he still did some despicable things, along with his own associates, in rubbing out Holt Warren, running off the Palfrey owners, and coming after us."

"George said he was sure they came to kill first and ask no questions. I thought perhaps it was the best way for him to tell it afterwards."

"I don't blame him for running. If my horse had been saddled, I would have been right behind him."

"But would you have left someone to fend for himself?"

"Oh, I don't think so. After all, I had a gun. I could have helped someone else."

"I was sorry about Mr. Simms."

"So was I. There was no need for it. As far as that goes, there was no need for any of this. As I see it, it all came out of a rotten man's will to take what he could get and to think he should get away with it. Some people might say that it comes from the evil in men's souls, but to borrow a phrase from a person who knew him, a person might wonder if that man had a soul."

"Everyone has a soul," said Tess.

"I won't argue that, just like I won't argue about whether people are born good, bad, or with a clean slate. I won't argue whether we all have a fair chance. But for those of us who do, and who want to make it through life with a clear conscience, it's repulsive to see someone who has to cheat and use force."

"I agree with you, and I hope it's all done now. It should be."

"I think it is."

"What do you think you will do next?"

He appreciated her changing the subject. "The deputy has asked me not to leave for a few days, but I expect to stay around a little longer anyway. I believe I've had enough of the work at the Palfrey, and I think your uncle and his friends will take the lumber that's in the stack and be done with it."

"That seems to be his line of thinking."

"So that leaves me free to help you bring in the rest of the potatoes and whatever comes next, like the pumpkins."

"And after that?"

"Well, I was hoping you and I might sketch out some notes on the same page."

"You have good ideas," she said as she moved toward him.

He closed his eyes, and for the second time, they kissed under the stars on the edge of the prairie.

ABOUT THE AUTHOR

John D. Nesbitt lives in the plains country of Wyoming, where he is Professor Emeritus of English and Spanish at Eastern Wyoming College. He writes western, contemporary, mystery, and retro/noir fiction as well as nonfiction and poetry. John has won many awards for his work, including four awards from the Wyoming State Historical Society (for fiction), two awards from Wyoming Writers for encouragement of other writers and service to the organization, two Wyoming Arts Council literary fellowships (one for fiction, one for nonfiction), two Western Fictioneers Peacemaker awards, four Peacemaker Finalist awards, six Will Rogers Medallion Awards, four Spur awards from Western Writers of America, and two Spur finalist awards. His most recent books are *Great Lonesome* and *Silver Grass*, frontier novels with Five Star. Visit his website at www.johnd nesbitt.com.

The employees of Five Star Publishing hope you have enjoyed this book.

Our Five Star novels explore little-known chapters from America's history, stories told from unique perspectives that will entertain a broad range of readers.

Other Five Star books are available at your local library, bookstore, all major book distributors, and directly from Five Star/Gale.

Connect with Five Star Publishing

Website:
gale.com/five-star

Facebook:
facebook.com/FiveStarCengage

Twitter:
twitter.com/FiveStarCengage

Email:
FiveStar@cengage.com

For information about titles and placing orders:
(800) 223-1244
gale.orders@cengage.com

To share your comments, write to us:
Five Star Publishing
Attn: Publisher
10 Water St., Suite 310
Waterville, ME 04901